KU-778-478

AN ALIEN STOLE MY PLANET

Illustrated by Allen Fatimaharan

MACMILLAN CHILDREN'S BOOKS

Published 2023 by Macmillan Children's Books
an imprint of Pan Macmillan
The Smithson, 6 Briset Street, London EC1M 5NR
EU representative: Macmillan Publishers Ireland Ltd,
1st Floor, The Liffey Trust Centre, 117-126 Sheriff Street Upper
Dublin 1, D01 YC43
Associated companies throughout the world
www.panmacmillan.com

ISBN 978-1-5290-7072-9

1 3 5 7 9 8 6 4 2

A CIP catalogue record for this book is available from the British Library.

Printed and bound by CPI Group (UK) Ltd, Croydon CR0 4YY
Designed by Suzanne Cooper

For the inventors,
makers and daydreamers.
P.P.

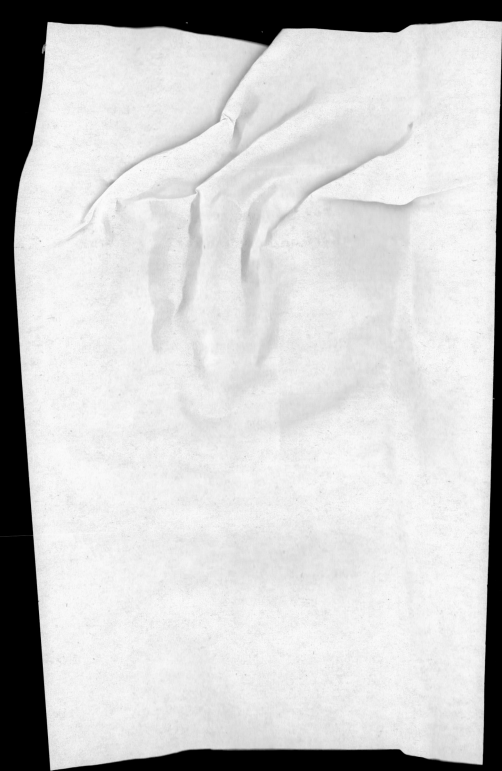

An Important Note From The Author

Before you start reading, there are a few things you should know:

① I, Esha Verma, am a **genius inventor** extraordinaire.

② I like lists.

③ It is my dream of ULTIMATE DREAMS to win the Young Inventor of the Year contest — and the mind-bogglingly brilliant, much-wanted **Brain Trophy.**

MADE FROM SUPER-COOL ZIRBOONIUM

④ This is my **THIRD** genius inventing journal.

⑤ You should only keep reading if you have read my first two genius journals.

⑥ If you have not, I will know and this book will SELF-DESTRUCT in exactly ten seconds (you have been warned).

⑦ My apprentice, Broccoli (aka James Bertha Darwin), was about to add something here, but I'm not sure what it was because he's disappeared to help change his new baby brother's nappy **(MEGA GROSS).**

I have told him we need to invent a nappy-changing device **URGENTLY** (a **NOSE PEG** is absolutely not enough protection).

⑧ Anyway. What you should definitely know is that my latest inventing adventure, which you are about to read about in this journal, was a *slight* disaster.

HOWEVER . . .

(9) It was absolutely **NOT** my fault that an alien almost **STOLE** Earth and everyone on it (yes, that includes you). It was just one of those things.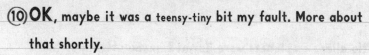

(10) **OK**, maybe it was a teensy-tiny bit my fault. More about that shortly.

[A note from Broccoli: Before I left to change the nappy, I was going to tell Esha that we cannot send out self-destructing books for health-and-safety reasons, so you can ignore that part. As you probably know by now, she can be a little dramatic.]

A Second Important
Note From The Author

No aliens or planets were harmed in the writing of this book.

Promise.

Where It All Went Wrong

I suppose I should start from the moment it all went wrong, AKA When Esha Verma Got into the Biggest Trouble of Her LIFE. If you, the Reader, have read my second important journal (which you should have), you will know *exactly* what I'm talking about – the ~~catastrophe~~ accident at the Central Research Laboratory.

And OK, *I know* I took Nishi's tickets to the laboratory without her permission (believe me, it was necessary), and *I know* things didn't turn out quite as planned (you should have seen the laboratory after) and *I know* that my family were pretty unhappy with me.

But . . . as I explained to Mum and Dad once we were all home, everything that happened at the Central Research Laboratory was an UNFORTUNATE INCIDENT.

'Unfortunate incidents,' I told them, 'are PART of inventing.

Look at Edison. Look at Mary Anderson. Look at Einstein. Without unfortunate

$E=mC^2$

incidents, **genius inventors** wouldn't be . . . well, **GENIUS INVENTORS.** It's all part of the process.'

For some reason my parents did not see it that way.

Instead, Mum turned as purple as a beetroot and said, 'Esha Verma, that was your **LAST CHANCE.** We warned you what would happen if you had one more inventing accident. But you didn't listen and now look what's happened! You almost destroyed that laboratory and you ruined things for your sister. Your father and I are **VERY** disappointed in you. Isn't that right, dear?' She looked at Dad.

Dad, who was nose-deep in his Sudoku, said, 'Yes, absolutely. What your mum says, Esha. Very disappointed. Extremely.'

Then Mum said the words that I had been *dreading.* Words that sent an **ICY COLD** shiver down my spine and filled me with a feeling of **DOOM** from head to toe.

'I'm sorry to say that you've left us with no choice. From now on, Esha, you are _**BANNED**_ from inventing.'

The words flew around the walls of the living room like a swarm of angry bees.

BANNED

FROM

INVENTING.

I am sure that you, the Reader, are probably thinking this was the moment that I, Esha Verma, **genius inventor**, launched into a stirring and eye-wateringly moving speech that showed Mum and Dad just how wrong they were and persuaded them to immediately reverse their ban on inventing. Unfortunately, coming up with stirring and eye-wateringly moving speeches is harder than you might expect. They are even harder when you have to think of them **ON THE SPOT**. Instead, what happened next was this:

STUNNED
INTO SILENCE

END OF THE WORLD

'I expect you to hand over your *Inventor's Handbook*,' continued Mum. 'And you're not allowed to use your room as an Inventor's HQ any more.'

(Talk about being **DRAMATIC**.)

'You will also not be allowed to enter the Young Inventor of the Year contest.'

'But – but—' I stammered. 'But what about the Brain Trophy? I really think this could be my year to win it!'

'You should have thought about that before you stole your sister's tickets and lied your way into the Central Research Laboratory.'

 Nishi, who was standing behind Mum, folded her arms across her chest and gave me a smirk that would have made a snake proud.

'No **Brain Trophy** and no inventing,' declared Mum, her eyes drilling into me like lasers. 'I will also be speaking to Broccoli's parents to make sure they know about this. Do you understand, Esha Verma?'

I opened my mouth to tell Mum that:

> No, I absolutely DID NOT understand. Do you even want me to become a genius inventor, renowned through all of history and beyond, because I'm 110% certain that no other inventor had ever had to put up with a family as ANNOYING as mine!

But Mum was looking at me with her most dangerous not-to-be-messed-with face, so, instead, I closed my mouth and nodded.

That was a few months ago.

Now, dear Reader, you must be thinking that this was it. **THE END.**

There was no way I could win the **Brain Trophy** now.

BANNED

I'd handed over my *Inventor's Handbook* and been **BANNED** from inventing. So had Broccoli.

In fact, you may already be getting ready to close this book and walk away in disappointment.

Well, DON'T!

After all, you're forgetting that I, Esha Verma, am a **genius inventor** extraordinaire and the *Inventor's Handbook* says that *the best inventors should* always *find a way to turn even the trickiest of situations to their ADVANTAGE.* I wasn't going to let anything or anyone stop me from creating a **MIND-BOGGLING** invention that would **bamboozle** the GENIE judges (the supreme brains of Genius & Extraordinary Inventions Inc), win the **Brain Trophy** and prove to my family just how GENIUS I was once and for all.

Stay tuned to find out exactly what happened.

[A note from Broccoli: Sadly, things didn't turn out quite as we hoped.]

~~Our Latest Genius Invention~~

Broccoli has interrupted again to say that I can't tell you about our BRAIN BOGGLING, TOE-TINGLING,

eye-popping 👀

GENIUS invention

until I've told you about the purple-spotted envelope that arrived and kick-started this whole thing.

I've just pointed out that his baby brother looks like he's about to puke.

[A note from Broccoli: Sorry about that, Reader. My VOM-TOM warning system is still not working quite as it should be.]

The Purple-Spotted Envelope

As I was saying . . .

The purple-spotted envelope arrived on a bright, sunny morning.

It was, I thought, as I munched my cereal, a perfect day to invent something that would win us the **Brain Trophy**. Annoyingly, I was having to work in secret. Even more annoyingly, Mum had decided to carry out 'spot checks' on my room to be doubly sure I *wasn't* inventing in **secret** (yawn-boring-yawn).

This meant I had no choice but to take **EVASIVE ACTION.**

EVASIVE ACTION 1: Find an alternative Inventor's HQ (I was already on this — as you'll find out).

EVASIVE ACTION 2: Hide any and all inventions and items related to inventing (if you, the Reader, should ever find yourself in this situation, I recommend unusual places where nobody would think to look).

EVASIVE ACTION 3: Be on my best behaviour at all times to avoid suspicion (this was proving irritating but necessary).

As soon as I'd finished breakfast, I sped up to my room and pulled my backup *Inventor's Handbook* out from a sock mountain (that's right – I had a backup. After a dinosaur had eaten my first one, I'd decided to keep a spare). I stuck it inside my English book, then I crept past the living room (where Mum was talking to Aunty Usha about begonias and cousin Binda's wedding) and opened the front door.

'I'm going to Broccoli's to work on my English homework!' I shouted. 'See you later!'

'Esha . . .' called Mum's warning voice through the door.

'Yes, I know,' I said. 'No inventing! Broccoli's banned too, remember?'

I banged the door shut. Then I waited a moment and silently sprinted back into the kitchen, through the garden and let myself into the garden shed.

The garden shed – AKA my alternative

INVENTOR'S HQ.

Now you, the Reader, may be wondering why, of all places, I had chosen our shed to build my secret inventions. There were, in fact, four good reasons:

1. Mum doesn't like spiders. **NOT ONE BIT.**
2. The shed was **full** of spiders. Therefore, it was the last place she would look for me.
3. Nishi had refused to enter the shed ever since a **giant** wasp had stung her on the nose (I am sure she deserved it).
4. Dad was supposed to have tidied the shed months ago. Fortunately, Dad's football team, Burnley FC, were doing surprisingly well this year, so he'd been too busy to even think about the shed. This meant it was the safest place I could invent in secret without anyone hearing or seeing me.

I'd only just taken out my *Inventor's Handbook* when I heard a knock on the shed door.

I froze.

There was another knock.

Tap-tap-tappity-tap-tap.

The Inventor's Code.

I breathed out in relief and inched open the door. Broccoli blinked back at me, his grumpy-looking tortoise, Archibald, held in his arms. (Archibald had been a sour-face ever since Broccoli had found out that he was going to be a big brother.)

[A note from Broccoli: Archibald has never been a sour-face in his entire life.]

'You're late,' I said. 'Did you check that nobody saw you?'

Broccoli nodded. 'Twice. Then I checked again to make triply sure.' He brushed a few dandelions off his jumper. 'I don't like all this sneaking around. And I *really* don't like squeezing through your fence.' He sneezed, bits of dandelion fluff whizzing out of his nose. 'That hole is tiny.' Archibald, who had a stray weed hanging off the top of his head, snickered in irritation.

'We've talked about this, Broccoli,' I reminded him. 'It's a secret entrance. If we make it any bigger, someone's sure to notice. Besides, we don't have a choice. We're both banned from inventing, remember? If either of our

parents get even a whiff about us
entering the Young Inventor of the
Year contest, we'll be grounded for
the rest of **FOREVER**. Now, I have two very important
things to discuss with you.'

'Actually, so have I—' began Broccoli.

'Number One: the Inventor of the Year contest is on the
tenth of August, which means we only have eight weeks to
come up with an invention. So far, I have nothing. I even
tried the Upside-Down Pose for maximum brain-sparks
and I've still got zilch. Which leads me onto Number
Two: maybe having a proper Inventor's HQ would
help. This place needs fixing up a bit. Maybe that's why I'm
not getting any brain-sparks.'

Archibald made a noise that
sounded like, 'Or maybe that's just you.'

'That's great, Esha,' said Broccoli, shifting from one
foot to the other. 'But—'

'First, we have to fix our inventing worktop.'
I pointed at the wonky table, which now also
had a few additional holes thanks to
an unfortunate encounter between

Broccoli's Orange Marmalade Spray and the Glo-Pro (one of my more recent inventions, designed to shine with more bedazzling brightness than any torch or other light-illuminating device). 'Just look at it – it's like working on a *rollercoaster!*

Broccoli nodded. 'Sure, but Esha, I—'

'And we need to do something about the smell in here. It's nothing like the inspirational **whiff** of my sock mountains. I think we should—Wait, what's the matter with you?' I said, staring at Broccoli, who was now almost **dancing** on the spot.

'I've been trying to tell you! This came through the post,' he said, whipping out a purple-spotted envelope from his pocket. His face shone with excitement. 'My Letterbox Alert System did the trick! I got to it before Mum and Dad saw it. Told you it made sense to redirect all inventing communication to my house. Mum and Dad are too distracted with all this baby—'

'Broccoli,' I interrupted sharply. 'Who is the letter from?'

'Didn't I say? GENIE, of course!'

'GENIE?' I echoed shrilly, snatching the envelope off him. 'You're telling me that *now*?'

'Well, I *was trying* to—'

'Honestly, Broccoli. You really need to speak more quickly sometimes.'

I stared at the envelope for a moment,

a SPINGLY-TINGLY
spark of excitement

fluttering in my stomach.

'Go on,' said Broccoli, his snot trembling in anticipation. 'Open it.'

Archibald yawned rudely.

I turned the envelope over and slid my finger under the GENIE stamp on the back. A burst of rainbow confetti exploded into the air as I lifted the flap. I looked at Broccoli, my heart thudding.

Carefully, I slid out a crisp sheet of parchment, the faint whiff of plum crumble and custard wafting out with it.

A plum

Dear Genius inventor,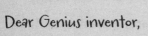

Some mind-bogglingly brilliant news! GENIE is celebrating its official half-century of bamboozling inventing excellence. To mark this special occasion, we would like to invite you to our once-in-a-lifetime Happy Half-Century Day on 10 July.

All of our guests can expect a jam-packed day of ultra-cool, ultra-awesome inventioning, which will also include the official Young Inventor of the Year contest.

'The contest?' exclaimed Broccoli, peering over my shoulder. 'But that's not meant to be for another two months!'

I turned the letter over.

That's right! We have decided to move the contest earlier than originally planned. In our experience, the best inventing is done under the tightest of time pressures, and we are certain that this new deadline will inspire you to create even better, even more brilliant inventions.

All genius inventors are requested to bring their entries to the judging room by 3 p.m. The winner of the Brain Trophy will be announced at a special ceremony at 5 p.m.

We look forward to welcoming you to our Half-Century Day. Further details, including the location of this momentous event and a map of the venue, are enclosed.

Happy inventing!

GENIE

I lowered the letter. The tenth of July. That left us only **four weeks** to come up with the **invention** of a **LIFETIME**.

I pulled out the map. 'Broccoli, look. The Half-Century Day is at Twiddle Manor – that's not far from here. We can get there ourselves without anyone finding out.'

'We'll need to work fast,' said Broccoli, 'if we've only got four weeks. We need . . .

inspiration!'

He whipped out his notebook with a fierce sniff. 'It's like the *Inventor's Handbook* says. Paragraph one, page thirty-four: *All genius inventors should keep an eye and ear out for inspiration at all times.* I think I'm getting the hang of it. Listen to this.' He cleared his throat.

'Idea One: Silent Lawnmowers. Date and time of inspiration: 8 June, 2.03 p.m. Location: Uncle Pete's garden.'

'Silent Lawnmowers?' I said. 'How on earth did you come up with that?'

'Mum said that babies need quiet,' explained Broccoli wisely.

'Babies?'

'Oh, yes,' he said, waving his notebook proudly at me. 'All of my current invention ideas are baby-inspired, in preparation for the arrival of Bertha Darwin Junior.'

Archibald made a rude noise at the back of his throat as if he was about to be sick.

Broccoli looked thoughtful. 'We still haven't decided on his name.'

'Broccoli—' I began slowly.

'Idea Two: The Baby-Food Masher — a fully automated masher! Designed to make *any and all food* suitable for babies. Including popcorn, asparagus and tinned peaches. Date and time of inspiration: 3 May, 11.31 a.m. Location: the kitchen.'

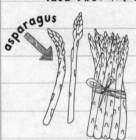

asparagus

'I don't think—'

'This is my best one yet — Idea Three: the Snot Scarf. Guaranteed to help you out of every snotty situation.'

He sniffed. 'It can wipe your nose *and* keep it warm. I thought it might be useful if Bertha Darwin Junior has a nose like mine—'

'Broccoli!' I interrupted. 'Those ideas are all – uh . . .'

He blinked at me expectantly.

'. . . an excellent start,' I said slowly.

Archibald guffawed, his shell shaking with laughter.

'But this is the **Brain Trophy**, remember? There is only

ONE ⟵ in ALL of existence

and, in case you're forgetting, it's made from Zirboonium, which was found in a meteorite that fell to Earth from space. That means the trophy is NOT OF THIS WORLD. Which means we need something – well – OUT of this world to win it. Something unexpected, something extraordinary. Like a time machine. Or a RoarEasy. Or—'

'Or a walking, talking robot?' said Broccoli.

I scowled. I absolutely did **NOT** need reminding that Ernie Rathbone had won last year's **Brain Trophy** with his robot, 2.0. Luckily he'd moved to another school a few months earlier, so I no longer had to see his **VICTORY SMIRK** every day.

'Four weeks,' I murmured, staring at the letter again. I chewed my lip, my brain cells *whirring*. 'Four weeks to come up with something

out of this world.'

'What about my Orange Marmalade Spray?' said Broccoli. 'Guaranteed to mask stinky sock fumes and sweeten the air with a unique marmalade aroma.' He smacked his lips together. 'One of the best smells in the entire world.'

I raised an eyebrow. 'You mean the extremely unstable Marmalade Spray that I specifically told you **NOT** to test when we were trialling the illuminance levels of the Glo-Pro?'

Broccoli cleared his throat. 'Well—'

'The same Orange Marmalade Spray that you accidentally dropped into the Glo-Pro? The same Marmalade Spray that caused an **explosion** that would have sent this shed shooting into outer space if we hadn't stopped it in time? *That* Marmalade Spray?'

'It's a work in progress,' said Broccoli, folding his arms across his chest. 'It just needs a few tweaks.'

I opened my mouth to say something extremely RUDE, then I thought better of it. 'No. There has to be something else. We just need to channel some inspiration.'

Broccoli's face lit up. 'Inspiration! I can do that.' He stretched his left arm straight in the air and shut his eyes, **wiggling** his fingers slowly.

'Broccoli, what are you doing?' I said impatiently.

'Channelling inspiration,' he explained, opening one eye. 'Chapter 45 of the *Inventor's Handbook*.'

'I'm not sure that's quite what we—'

'James!' called a man's voice from the direction of Broccoli's garden.

'That's Dad!' Broccoli hissed. He ducked under the

Inventor's Worktop like a rocket.

'He can't see you in here, anyway,' I pointed out.

'Oh – yes – I know that,' said Broccoli. He cleared his
throat and stood up again.

 Archibald snickered.

'I thought you said nobody
saw you come through the fence.'

'James!'

'They didn't,' said Broccoli. 'I'm <u>100%</u> sure of it.'

I climbed onto the Inventor's Worktop and peered
through the dirt-stained window. 'If you're 100% sure, why
is your dad near the secret entrance?'

Broccoli flushed. 'Well – 90% sure. Give or take.'

I groaned. 'Broccoli! You did hide the secret entrance,
didn't you?'

He nodded, his snot **wobbling**. 'There's no way he'll
see it. I covered it back up again with leaves. It's
practically invisible . . .'

I gasped.

Because, dear Reader, that was
the moment that **GENIUS
INSPIRATION** struck.

The moment that sent a spark of

FIZZY-WHIZZY FANTASTICNESS

shooting through me.

The moment that lit up my **BRAIN CELLS**
☆**brighter**☆ than a Holi festival.

Suddenly I knew. With the same
knowingness that I'd felt when I had the
brain-spark for the time machine and
the **RoarEasy**, I knew EXACTLY what to invent.

'James?' I watched as Broccoli's dad peered round his
garden in puzzlement. Then he scratched his chin and
disappeared inside.

'He's gone,' I said, leaping off the worktop. I whirled
Broccoli around on the spot. 'And you've just given me the
most STUPENDOUS idea!'

Archibald made a noise that sounded like, 'Not again.'

'I have?'

'Our invention, Broccoli! The MIND-BLOWING idea we
need. It's total **genius!**'

'It is?' He paused. 'What is?'

29

'An invisibility

device, of course! That's what will win

us the **Brain Trophy!** Don't you see it?'

'Well, if it's an invisibility device, then probably not—'

'It's a **STUPENDOUS** spark of brilliance, Broccoli!

STU-PEN-DOUS! We'll invent the device, make ourselves

invisible, go to **GENIE**'s Half-Century Day and reveal

ourselves in style, at precisely 3 p.m. The judges will be so

STUNNED they won't even need to see the other inventions.

They'll just hand the **Brain Trophy** over to us

immediately.' I swept my hand through the air in a

grand magician's flourish. 'Say it with me, Broccoli.

"In-vis-i-bil-i-ty."'

'In-vis-ibility?' echoed Broccoli hesitantly.

Archibald made a noise that sounded like, 'Of all the

human pets, why did I have to get this one?'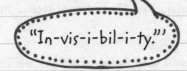

'That's it!' I grinned. 'Can you feel it now? That

SPINGLY-TINGLY spark? **Can you feel it** h^oppⁱng and

bu_zzⁱng inside you?'

'Um. I'm not sure.'

'Inventor's instinct, Broccoli. Trust me on this. We'll win the **Brain Trophy** before Bertha Darwin Junior arrives. And when we win, our parents will FINALLY realize that they were wrong to ever ban us from inventing. We'll be able to restart our

important genius work. In a proper Inventor's HQ. No more sneaking around.'

Broccoli glanced down at his notebook. I hesitated.

'But . . . if you really want to invent a Silent Lawnmower, we can do that instead,' I said slowly.

'Really?' said Broccoli, sounding surprised.

'We're a team, remember?' I said firmly. 'Whatever we invent, we'll do it together.'

Broccoli continued to stare at his notebook. 'You *really* think this In-vis-ibility device is more likely to win us the **Brain Trophy** than a Silent Lawnmower?' he said. 'Or a Snot Scarf?'

'I don't think so – I *know* so, Broccoli! This is the invention that will win us the **Brain Trophy**. I can feel it in my BONES.'

'Inventor's instinct?' said Broccoli.

'Inventor's instinct,' I said solemnly.

Broccoli thought for a moment longer, then he flipped his notebook shut. 'An In-vis-ibility device it is,' he said.

'Really?'

He grinned. 'The Silent Lawnmower can wait until Bertha Darwin Junior arrives. Get your Inventor's Kit together,

Esha. We only have four weeks until the contest and we have LOTS of work to do.'

How We Invented the Inviz-Whiz: Our Top-Secret Method...

... will remain top secret.

Unless you can solve the following invisible riddle:

[A note from Broccoli: What I can tell you is that it involved DAYS of sneaking around, almost getting caught (twice) and an unfortunate encounter with Nishi and a bag of rambutans.]

The Portal in the Shed

There it was.

At last.

The mind-bogglingly **BRILLIANT** result of all our hard work. The Inviz-Whiz.

(No, I am **NOT** going to describe it to you in detail because my design is top secret – obviously.)

I placed it on the Inventor's Worktop and took a deep breath. Today was the day – the day we trialled and tested the invention. The day we found out if it _really worked_ (which it would).

And also . . . the day of **GENIE's** Half-Century Day and the contest.

Now, I know what you're thinking, and you're right. In an ideal situation, we would have tested the invention weeks before the competition. But it had taken longer to build the Inviz-Whiz than I'd hoped. In fact, it had taken so long that we were **ALMOST OUT OF TIME.**

I glanced at the clock. 11 a.m. In precisely six hours, GENIE would announce the winner of the **Brain Trophy.**

That gave us only **FOUR HOURS** to trial *and* test the Inviz-Whiz, check and correct any (unlikely) errors, make ourselves invisible and take it to GENIE's Half-Century Day in time for the judging.

'Then we change the world,' I whispered. 'This is it. This is really it—'

Tap-tap-tappity-tap-tap.

And there, right on time, was Broccoli.

Before I could move, the door to the shed burst open.

'I told you to let me go first!' huffed Broccoli as a small, freckle-faced ~~irritant~~ boy charged inside. He looked around the shed and twisted his face in the most spectacular nose wrinkle I had ever seen.

'*Bean?*' I said.

A Short (but Not Sweet) Interruption about Bean:

1. Bean's real name is, in fact, Oliver Betty Darwin (Betty is Broccoli's great-grandmother).

2. He is Broccoli's cousin (regrettably).

3. He does not go anywhere without his slingshot.

4. The last time he visited Broccoli, he **SABOTAGED** three of our genius inventions, including the Self-Knitting Needles (a **genius inventor** may forgive, but they **DO NOT FORGET**).

5. He is the **MOST** annoying seven-year-old to ever exist **ON THE PLANET.**

'What is this **STINKPIT?**' he declared.

'Stinkpit? This is our Inventor's HQ,' I said, glaring at him.

'This? *Gross-a-RAMA.*'

'It's temporary,' I said, giving Broccoli a YOU'D BETTER EXPLAIN YOURSELF NOW look.

'He came over with Aunt Wendy last night,' said Broccoli glumly. 'She's staying with Mum until the baby comes. I've been asked to look after him.'

Bean snorted. 'I don't need looking after.' He folded his arms across his chest and glowered at both of us. 'I'm seven years old, which means I'm practically an adult. I can take care of myself.'

I'm **7**

Broccoli sighed. 'I'm supposed to make sure he doesn't get in trouble. Aunt Wendy said it will be good practice for when Bertha Darwin Junior comes along.'

'Babies are **BOR-ING,**' said Bean. 'Just like your pet.' He made a face at Archibald, who stiffened. 'Tortoises are the most **BOR-ING** creatures on the entire planet.'

Archibald's eyes thinned. He made a noise that sounded like, 'Watch yourself, human worm.'

'I can't believe you two are still inventing. **BORING**. How long do we have to stay here? Why is that table full of holes?'

'None of your business,' I said. 'And *you* are not staying here another second. Broccoli, you have to take him back to your house. We have imporṭaṇṭ work to do, remember?' I looked pointedly at the clock.

Broccoli sniffed, looking sorry for himself. 'I can't. I promised Aunt Wendy. She thinks I'll be a good influence on him.'

'**BOR-ING,**' said Bean again. 'There's no way I want to be like you, Broccoli bore-brain.

DOUBLE
BOR-ING.

And by the way, your secret entrance stinks.'

'You showed him the secret entrance?' I said, scowling at Broccoli.

He flushed. 'How else was I supposed to bring him here?'

EURGH.

I checked the clock. 11.05 a.m. We now had *less* than four hours left to trial and test the Inviz-Whiz *and* get it to **GENIE's** Half-Century Day by the 3 p.m. deadline. 'FINE. We don't have time for this. Just keep him out of the way. And *you*,' I said, snatching the Inviz-Whiz away from Bean, who was peering at it.

'DON'T TOUCH ANYTHING.
UNDERSTAND?'

Bean pretended to yawn. Then he took a marshmallow out of his pocket and slid it into his slingshot.

'**BEAN!**' said Broccoli. 'You can't throw marshmallows around in here.'

'Marshmallows?' said Bean, looking offended. 'These aren't just marshmallows. These are

modified marshmallows. Specially designed by me to create the best slingshot projectile. Ultra-sleek, ultra-streamlined, ultra-superior.'

BLOP! The marshmallow whizzed across the air and hit Broccoli square on his forehead.

'**OW!**' said Broccoli. 'That hurt, Bean!'

'That's what you call a perfect bullseye,' sniggered Bean.

'You do that again and I'm telling Aunt Wendy.'

Bean made a face. 'Has anyone ever told you that you're a **TOTAL BORE?**'

Archibald made a noise that sounded like, 'Only I call him that, brain of toad.'

Broccoli flushed. 'I AM NOT a total bore! I am, in fact—'

'Could you two please keep quiet?' I snapped, clutching the Inviz-Whiz. I flicked the switch to ON. 'This is a crucial moment in the inventing process.'

'What's the whistle for?' sneered Bean rudely.

'This isn't a whistle,' I retorted. 'This is the Inviz-Whiz. Designed to turn the user INVISIBLE.'

'Bet it doesn't.'

'It does,' I said.

'How do you know?'

'Because,' I said, 'I am a **genius inventor** and I know things.'

'Says who?'

I decided to ignore him. After all, it didn't matter what Bean said. We'd done our research. We'd checked, double-checked and triple-checked the blueprint. The Inviz-Whiz would work. I was **110%** certain of it. This time, NOTHING was going to stop us winning the **Brain Trophy**. And after I won, Mum and Dad would see that they were wrong to ever doubt my inventing brilliance. In fact, they'd probably drop on their knees and BEG me to forgive them for being so OBLIVIOUS to their daughter's genius.

I put the silver end of the Inviz-Whiz to my mouth.

'Go for it, Esha,' whispered Broccoli.

Closing my eyes, I blew as hard as I could.

CHEEEEEHHHHHHEEEEEEEEEEEPPPPPPPP!

A shrill trill rang through the air. My skin prickled. A shiver ran down my spine. I opened my eyes. By my genius calculations, this was it. This was the moment I'd been waiting for. At last, I was—

 'I can still see you,' said Bean, sounding bored out of his skull.

AH.

'Are you sure that was the right end?' said Broccoli.

I nodded. 'Silver to become invisible. Blue to reverse.'

'**BOR-ING**,' said Bean.

Suddenly the shed's single lightbulb crackled.

I glanced up with a frown. 'Maybe it's a delayed effect.'

Bean yawned loudly. '*Maybe your invention doesn't*
work.'

Before I could reply, a cluster of purple and golden
sparks appeared in front of us, perfectly
suspended in the air.

*Now that was interesting. Where had
they come from?*

'Uh – Esha?' said Broccoli. He stepped back so quickly
that he trod on Bean, who jumped back with an angry yelp.
'That wasn't in our calculations, was it?'

'Well, no,' I said. 'But I think it's a good sign.'

The cloud of sparks began to move.

They spun round and round,
faster and faster,
until there was a beautiful bright
circle of sparkly-crackly light
floating in the air. Then –

BOOM!

I was flung suddenly back onto a mattress. The Inviz-Whiz flew out of my hand and landed on the floor, where it rolled under the table.

'Ow –' I groaned as I sat up – 'that wasn't what—'

But I forgot what I was going to say next because of what I saw in front of me. Or rather, what I **COULDN'T** see.

Where there had been a spinning circle of light, there was now a

SPINNING, CRACKLING HOLE.

Through the hole I could see . . . something. Something that was very definitely **NOT** the shed.

Something that looked a bit like this:

UH OH.

A silvery-green light shone through the hole, illuminating the shed like an aquarium. On the other side of the hole I could just make out what appeared to be purple rock.

'What was that?' said Bean, untangling himself from a pile of sleeping bags. His eyes were shining. 'Can we do it ag—

WHOAH!'

He breathed in sharply as he caught sight of the hole.

He took a step towards it.

'Stay back, Bean!' said Broccoli. He leapt to his feet and whipped his arm in front of his cousin. Archibald poked his head out of his shell, his face lighting up with excitement as he saw the hole.

'We shouldn't get any closer until we know what that is,' said Broccoli.

'Don't you know anything?' said Bean incredulously. 'That's a **portal**. And that –' he waved his hand at the peculiar purple rock on the other side – 'that is somewhere else. Somewhere that is not here.'

(What did I tell you? Most annoying seven-year-old on the planet.)

'Bet you it's Australia,' said Bean.

'Australia isn't **purple**,' I said.

'We should **explore**,' said Bean.

'No, we should not,' said Broccoli firmly. 'That could be
 anywhere, and until we have any further
information, **no one is exploring**.
Do you understand?'

'*No one is exploring*,' mimicked Bean. 'You're more
boring than a—'

'**SSH!**' I interrupted. I leaned forward,
cupping a hand to my ear. 'Listen. Can you
hear that?'

In the distance, I could make out a faint noise.

SCHLUP-SCHLUP.

It sounded . . . **slimy**.

'Sounds like a slug,' said Bean.

'**A GIANT slug**.'

'Shhh,' I **hissed**. 'I think it's getting closer.'

SCHLUP-SCHLUP.

SCHLUP-SCHLUP.

'Let go!' said Bean, tugging impatiently against Broccoli
who was now holding onto his arm.

SCHLUP-SCHLUP.

It (**was**) getting **closer**.

'Esha, we need to close that thing,' said Broccoli. He nodded at the Inviz-Whiz, which was still lying on the floor. 'Try that. If the silver end opened that circle, the blue end might close it.'

SCHLUP-SCHLUP.
SCHLUP-SCHLUP.

I hesitated.

OK, I wasn't invisible  – but still, it wasn't every day that a portal opened up in your shed. I couldn't help thinking that Bean was possibly a teensy-tiny bit right. Surely it wouldn't do any harm to have a quick look at what was on the other side of that hole?

'Esha!' gasped Broccoli, his face red with the effort of holding onto Bean. '**Close. It.**

Now.'

SCHLUP-SCHLUP.
SCHLUP-SCHLUP.

'OK, OK,' I muttered. Slowly, I turned to reach for the Inviz-Whiz. But before I could pick it up, a shape blocked out the hole's silvery-green light. A second later,

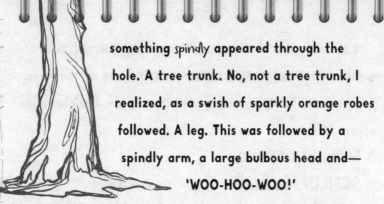

something *spindly* appeared through the hole. A tree trunk. No, not a tree trunk, I realized, as a swish of sparkly orange robes followed. A leg. This was followed by a spindly arm, a large bulbous head and—

'WOO-HOO-WOO!'

Whatever-it-was suddenly slipped and toppled through the hole into the shed with a loud **CRASH**. Then, with a **SCHLUP-SCHLUP,** the creature stood up,

TOWERING

over us in a

supremely sticky

spectacle of slime.

An Official Apology from Broccoli to Earth

Dear Earth and its readers, I would like to take this moment to apologize for everything that happens next.

In fact, thinking about it, now is your chance to close this book and continue with your life in happy ignorance, never knowing how close you came to annihilation.

Really.

There is no need for you to continue reading. In fact, it might be best if you don't.

If you **do** insist on reading on, then all I will say is sorry again. It really was an accident.

Thanks and very best,

Broccoli

The Visitor from the Newporla Dimension

My inventor's instincts twitched to RED ALERT as I stared at the slimy figure in front of us.

Like the government, NASA and the Secret Service (who all interviewed us afterwards), I am sure that you, the Reader, are also foot-hoppingly desperate to know what the visitor looked like – so I have included the picture I gave them.

Bean gasped.

Archibald stared at the visitor in delight and made a noise that sounded like, 'Finally, something interesting to tell Pa.'

Broccoli made a peculiar noise and stepped back, dragging his cousin with him.

I goggled. Forget begging my forgiveness. Mum and Dad would be absolutely FUMING when they discovered I had let a mysterious visitor into the shed.

The creature looked around, its enormous eyes making a soft, wet sound as it blinked. The antenna on top of its head whirred and flashed a bright yellow. It said something that sounded a bit like, 'Grolly-eyzy-iggli-ffttsshy-o-o-bo.' Or maybe it was, 'Grobby-ezzy-eegli-ppptshy-o-o-po.' (It really was impossible to know for sure.)

'Who are you?' said Bean.

The antenna flashed twice.

When the visitor spoke again, I could understand.

'Planet identified: Earth.'

Its voice sounded **squelchy** and **deep**, as if it had swallowed a trombone.

'Species identified: Earthling. Language identified:

English.' The creature's mouth **stretched** into a wide grin, the flap on its chin **wobbling** with glee. 'I am here. Har-Har-Har. I am really here. Har-Har-Har.'

OK, I am sure that you, the Reader, are probably wondering why I did not *sprint* express style out of the shed, but remember Secondus Secondi? Today was not the first time I had encountered a <u>mysterious</u> visitor from . . . elsewhere (actually, I still wasn't **100%** sure where Secondus was from). I was practically a total **EXPERT** at dealing with these kinds of situations.

[A note from Broccoli: I'm not sure if *expert* is quite the right word.]

So I was certain I could deal with this one.

Clearing my throat, I put my hands on my hips and looked at the creature with my most **FEARSOME** expression.

'Excuse me,' I said, 'but who exactly are you and what are you doing in my shed?'

'Esha,' whispered Broccoli hoarsely, still gripping Bean. 'I don't think you should be talking—'

'Earthling,' the creature went on in its **DEEP DRONE**. 'Har-Har-Har. Punier than I expected.' It looked at each of us in turn – Broccoli, me and Bean.

'Puny, **punier**, puniest.'

'I asked you a question,' I said. 'Two, in fact. Who are you and why are you in my shed?'

The creature looked disappointed. 'You do not recognize me?'

I shook my head.

'I am Goospa, the five-hundredth Prince of the Planet Zelpha, of the Triweeni Cluster in the Newporla Dimension. Exact co-ordinates: 3XYZ-890-12WEZ. Har-Har-Har. Do you recognize me now?'

I shook my head.

'An alien prince?' said Bean in delight. He pulled himself free from Broccoli and held his hand out to the visitor. 'Hello, Mr Goospa, Your Highness. I am Oliver Betty Darwin, otherwise known as Bean, and I am pleased to meet you.

Welcome to Earth. I would be happy to give you a tour of our planet.' He smiled widely. 'I am the **best** and cleverest of our human species.' He waved his hand at the hole. 'I told them it was a portal,' he continued smugly, 'but **they** didn't believe me. You really shouldn't waste your time with—'

'Bean,' hissed Broccoli. *'What are you doing?'*

'A tour?' echoed Goospa. 'Har-Har-Har. *Puny Earthling.* I am not here for a *tour.* Har-Har-Har.'

'No?' said Bean, sounding disappointed. He peered past Goospa towards the portal. 'Maybe you could give me a tour instead. Of your planet. Zelpha, you said? It looks very . . . purple. And interesting. Purple and interesting.'

Goospa blinked at the portal then back at him. 'That is not Zelpha, Earthling. Har-Har-Har. *That* is a different planet. I have travelled a long way to reach Earth.'

His arm suddenly shot out towards a shelf. Grabbing hold of a blue paint pot, he upended its contents into his mouth and gulped it down noisily. 'Tast-y. But not as tast-y as the earthly blue-berries.'

'Blueberries?' I said. 'Have you had Earthly blueberries?'

Globules of slimy spit whizzed into the air as Goospa smacked his lips. 'Only once,' he said dreamily. 'They are of course a rare delicacy so far from your planet. But the Earthly blue-berry is the best in all the galaxies, renowned and revered by our entire species. Now I am here, I can teleport Earth. The Ma and The Pa will be pleased.'

'Teleport Earth?' squeaked Broccoli. His snot dropped a little.

'Teleport Earth TO WHERE?'

'Back to Zelpha, of course. It will arrive in time for The Ma and The Pa's Grand Recrowning,' said Goospa. His chin wobbled, his eyes bright with glee. 'I will gift them the Earth and we will grow the Earthly blue-berry across your entire planet. Tast-y. Very tast-y.'

'Across the planet?' echoed Bean. He frowned. 'But I don't like blueberries.'

I stared at Goospa in complete bewilderment. Of all the reasons for a slimy alien to want Earth, blueberries wouldn't have been number one on my list. Or number two thousand, for that matter.

'The Pa and The Ma will have an endless supply of the Earthly blue-berry,' continued Goospa. 'Har-Har-Har. My four hundred and ninety-nine brothers and sisters will  bow to *me*. Har-Har-Har. Zelpha shall have a crown prince instead of a crown princess. At last. They will respect me. Har-Har-Har.'

My stomach did a horrible tumble-turn.

Forget what Mum and Dad would say. If Earth got zapped to another dimension, it wouldn't just be **me** in trouble. It would be the ENTIRE PLANET.

Now I know that you, the Reader, are probably thinking this was the perfect moment for a genius idea. Only it is difficult to think of genius ideas when you are faced with a squelchy slimeball who wants to **TELEPORT** your whole world for blueberries. Try it, if you don't believe me.

[A note from Broccoli: Or don't.]

Broccoli was sniffing loudly. Only it wasn't a single sniff, I realized suddenly. It was a sequence of sniffs.

Sniff-sniff-sniffly-sniff-sniff.

The Inventor's Code.

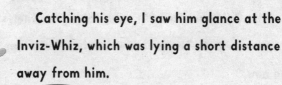

Catching his eye, I saw him glance at the Inviz-Whiz, which was lying a short distance away from him.

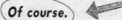 Of course.

We had to send Goospa back through the portal and use the Inviz-Whiz to close it.

'I think you've made a mistake, Mr Goospa,' I said, glancing across the shed for something I could use to give him a **GOODBYE NUDGE** through the portal.

'Let me introduce myself. My name is Esha Verma and I am a **genius inventor** extraordinaire. This is my apprentice, Broccoli.'

Out of the corner of my eye, I spotted a broom behind me. That could work.

'As **inventors,** we know that teleportation is currently impossible.' I stepped back, edging closer towards the broom. 'You won't be able to teleport Earth **anywhere.**'

'Puny Earthlings. You know nothing,' said Goospa. 'I shall build a teleportation device. Har-Har-Har. It shall be easy. Then, at precisely The Optimum Time, I will teleport Earth.'

'The Optimum Time?' I said, taking another stealthy step backwards. The broom was only a few steps away from me now.

'The Optimum Time. Today at exactly 3.30 p.m. on the Earthling hour, the galaxies will be perfectly aligned for planetary teleportation. Har-Har-Har. The clock is **tick-ticking**, Earthlings. Har-Har-Har.'

'Why don't you Earthling this?' retorted Bean.

With impressive speed, he slid a marshmallow into his slingshot and fired. It **TORPEDOED** across the air and **bounced** off Goospa's arm with a loud BLOP!

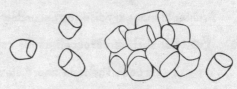

'You're not taking Earth **anywhere**. I won't let you!' BLOP! Another marshmallow hit Goospa's leg. 'I'm going to tell my mum! The government! I'll be a hero!' BLOP! 'And I *don't like blueberries!*' Another marshmallow whizzed through the air and pinged off Goospa's antenna.

UH OH.

Goospa looked down at the marshmallow, his almond eyes blinking slowly.

'You are incorrect, Earthling,' said Goospa. 'Har-Har-Har. You will tell nobody. Har-Har-Har.'

Before either of us could move, his arm shot out and wrapped itself around Bean.

'Har-Har-Har. Goodbye, Earthling.' With a quick flick of his slimy wrist, Goospa lifted Bean into the air and *threw him through the portal.*

Archibald made a noise that sounded like, 'Good riddance.'

'**Bean!**' shrieked Broccoli as his cousin **bounced** through the hole and disappeared from view. 'Bean, come—'

With another flick of his wrist, Goospa seized Broccoli's leg and flung *him* through the portal after Bean.

'BROCCOLI!'

I dived sideways for the Inviz-Whiz. I'd get Broccoli and Bean back — but protecting our invention was the priority. After all, it controlled the portal. As my fingers reached out towards the device, a cold, wet thing wrapped itself around my shoe.

'*LET ME GO!*' I bellowed.

Using my other leg, I lashed out at Goospa's arm. His grip loosened, just enough for me to slip free. With supreme **acrobatics**, I lunged towards the Inviz-Whiz again. Only I wasn't quite quick enough. Just as I seized hold of it, Goospa snatched it out of my grasp. With his other arm, he lifted me into the air so that I was hovering upside down, a few centimetres away from his face.

'Blue,' he said, eyeing one end of the Inviz-Whiz. 'Blue like the blue-berry.'

'Give that back!' I yelled. 'That's mine!'

Before I could stop him, Goospa threw the Inviz-Whiz into his mouth.

CHOMP CHOMP.

'Hm. Not as tast-y as the blue-berry.'

'You ate it!' I gasped. I couldn't believe what my eyes had just witnessed.

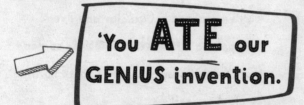

'You **ATE** our **GENIUS** invention.

That took us **WEEKS** of work! That was going to win us the **Brain Trophy!**'

[A note from Broccoli: Well . . . it was supposed to until it opened a portal instead.]

Goospa's eyes scanned me up and down.

'Esha-Verma. Verma-Esha. Inventor. Har-Har-Har.'

He smacked his lips, spraying **globules** of **slimy spit** onto my face. 'You will do, yes. You will do nicely.'

A horrible **shiver** crept down my spine.

Surely he didn't mean . . .

'Don't you even **THINK of eating me!**' I growled, giving him my most fierce **ESHA LASER GLARE.** My fingers scrabbled to undo the button on my Inventor's Kit (after losing everything **TWICE**, I had finally sewn one onto my dungarees. Unfortunately, this made it difficult to access my genius inventions quickly).

'I've escaped a *Guzzler* and I've stopped a **weathernova,** so don't think I can't stop *you*. And I taste nothing like blueberries!'

'Eat you?' Goospa blinked in surprise. 'Why would I eat you? Stringy, hairy Earthling. Yuck-yucky. No thank you. I do, however, have *another* use for you.' A chilling smile crept across his face. 'Goodbye, Esha-Verma-Verma-Esha.'

With one grand sweep, he flung me through the portal.

WHEEEEEEEEE!

A blast of cool air hit me as
I whizzed through it and landed,
with a **THUMP-THUNK,**
on hard, purple rock.

OW.

I **wobbled** to my feet with a loud groan.

'Check it out,' said Bean, shielding his eyes as he looked
into the distance. 'We're on a different *planet*—'

'Stop talking, Bean,' snapped Broccoli.

Archibald poked his head out of his shell, his
eyes widening as he looked past me.

'Esha,' gasped Broccoli. 'The portal. It's getting smaller!'

I swivelled round.

My heart dropped down to the bottom of my toes.

Broccoli was right. Some distance away from us, the
portal was

definitely,
absolutely,
shrinking.

'Oh no you don't!' I shouted, sprinting towards the portal. **'RUN, BROCCOLI!'**

My feet pounded against the ground as the portal shrivelled in front of me. Through it, I could see Goospa. Something was happening to him. He was **shaking** and *shivering*. A gleam of yellow light shone around his body.

I kept on running. But as I watched—

Goospa's head dropped into his neck, then his shoulders dropped downwards, almost as if he was

Shrinking into himself.

His arms and legs shot inwards with a horrible **POP-CRUNCH-POP!**

There was a flash of yellow light, so bright it hurt my eyes.

When I looked back at the circle, my feet stopped automatically. My jaw dropped.

Standing in the centre of the portal, looking right at me, was . . . (ME.)

Esha Verma. With the same pointy nose, the same ponytail with special rainbow-coloured inventioning hairband, the same inventioning dungarees.

UH OH.

Things had just got a

whole

lot

MORE

complicated.

I began to run again.

'Esha!' squeaked Broccoli as we sprinted forward. 'Esha, are you seeing this? He – he changed into you! There's **ANOTHER YOU** IN THE SHED!'

(As if I hadn't noticed.)

'OI!' I yelled. My breath pulled painfully in my chest as I raced forward. The portal fizzed and spat, the hole to the shed shrinking before my eyes. '**WHAT DO YOU THINK YOU'RE DOING? YOU CAN'T JUST become ME!** That's – that's – probably illegal! Or at least VERY RUDE! THERE'S ONLY ONE GENIUS ESHA VERMA IN THIS WORLD, SO YOU CAN JUST CHANGE RIGHT BACK AGAIN!'

Goospa smirked at me through the shrinking portal, a horrible, icy smirk that sent a shiver right into the deepest pit of my stomach. Then he held up a hand, *my* hand, and waved at me – as the portal, with a final crackle

of sparks, spiralled away into nothing.

Marooned

'*NO!*' I leapt forward, my fingers brushing air where the portal had been.

'It's gone,' wheezed Broccoli hoarsely, coming to a stop beside me. 'It's really gone.'

'You don't say, genius,' gasped Bean, bending down beside him. Two pink spots had formed on his cheeks. 'This is your fault, Broccoli. I had the situation under control.'

'*Control?*' huffed Broccoli. 'You were the first one to get thrown in! What made you think that *marshmallows* would stop him?'

'Modified marshmallows,' said Bean snootily. 'Besides, I'm not the one who opened a portal and let an ALIEN onto Earth.  I thought you were trying to turn yourselves invisible?'

'We were,' I said. 'I don't know what happened. Must have been something to do with the SPATIAL CIRCUITRY . . .'

'I don't understand,' said Broccoli, still staring at where the portal had been. 'How did it disappear like that?'

'Well – uh –' I cleared my throat – 'it might be because Goospa ate the Inviz-Whiz.'

Broccoli blinked. 'WHAT?'

Archibald made a noise that sounded like,
'Oh, you're in trouble now.'

'But that means –' Broccoli swallowed – 'without the Inviz-Whiz, we can't reopen the portal.' He breathed in sharply.

'Oh, this is bad.
This is TERRIBLE
WE'RE STUCK!'

'Stuck?' said Bean. 'On an alien planet?' He thought about this for a moment, then he grinned. 'Awesome.'

'No, this is not awesome,' retorted Broccoli, his snot shaking wildly. 'We don't even know where we are! Or how we're going to get back!'

'Pre-cisely!' said Bean. He danced away from us and

cartwheeled
across the purple rocky ground. 'This is our chance to have some **REAL FUN!**'

'Fun?' squeaked Broccoli. 'How is this fun?'

'We can have a proper adventure!' shouted Bean.

Archibald rolled his eyes and made a noise that sounded like, 'I would rather dance with a slug than have an adventure with you, enemy of tortoise.'

I looked around.

All I could see for MILES AND **MILES** was purple ROCK.

There was rock in front of us. Rock behind us. Rock to the left. More rock to the right.

It was as if we were standing on top of an **enormous** purple cabbage.

The only thing that wasn't purple was the sky. It was pink like candyfloss without a single cloud in sight. Flashes of green and silver light glimmered between the pink like butterflies.

Broccoli wrinkled his nose. 'What's that awful **smell?**'

He was right. There was a horrible sour smell. I picked
up a pebble and gave it a sniff. **'Eurgh!'** I threw
the pebble back down. 'I think it's the planet,'
I said. 'It smells like – like—'

'Curdled milk,' said Broccoli. 'Warm,
curdled milk.' He looked like he was
about to be sick.

'Right then,' I said.

(After all, one of us had to pull themselves together.)

'We might not know exactly what planet we're on, but
we know where we are *not*. One – we are definitely not on
Earth. Two – we are also not on Goospa's planet, Zelpha.
He told us that, remember?'

'Well, wherever we are, we have to find a way back,'
said Broccoli. 'If Goospa builds his teleportation device,
the whole Earth is in trouble.'

'I know that!' I said. I *also* knew that panicking
wasn't going to help anyone. Besides,
we'd dealt with wormholes,
weathernovas and dinosaurs.
I was quite certain we could
deal with a **slimy** alien.

With genius-level speed, I assessed the situation.

1. We were marooned on a mysterious alien planet, which appeared to be composed mostly of smelly purple rock (location still to be identified).

2. A shapeshifting alien had taken over my identity back on Earth.

3. The same shapeshifting alien was planning to steal Earth and teleport it back to their own planet.

4. As if that wasn't bad enough, we were stuck with **BEAN**.

Terrible didn't quite cover it. This was a

MEGA WHOPPER DISASTER.

I decided not to tell Broccoli that.

'Let's think like **genius inventors**,' I said brightly. 'What does Chapter 46 of the *Inventor's Handbook* say?'

'*A genius inventor is never really stuck*,' Broccoli said, his face screwed up in concentration, '*only temporarily stumped.*' He took a deep breath. 'Think like a **genius inventor**. OK. No reason to panic – not at all.'

He pulled out his notebook. 'We should start by taking an inventory of our inventions.'

I punched him lightly on the arm. 'See? You're thinking *exactly* like a **genius inventor**. Maybe we could use what we've got to create a new portal.' I checked my Inventor's Kit. 'Boomers. *Caramelizer Lollies*. The Ultra-Umbrella. Glo-Pro. The **Two-way Talkie**.'

(In case you, the Reader, are wondering, we had invented most of these in secret over the last few months. Impressive, I know.)

'And a bottle of Orange Marmalade Spray,' said Broccoli, checking his pocket.

We stared at the inventions in silence for a moment.

'I don't think any of these are going to help us create a new portal,' said Broccoli.

'No,' I said, chewing my lip.

'What about the Two-way Talkie? It has a dual comms system. We can use it to call for help.'

I shook my head. 'The second talkie is with Nishi, remember? She *stole* it after we dropped those rambutans in her wellies and she still hasn't given it back. Even if we can reach her, I guarantee she won't help us – she's still cross about *everything* that happened at the laboratory.'

(OK, maybe Nishi had a good reason, considering that we accidentally got her banned from the Central Research Laboratory for ever, but I wasn't going to admit that.)

'That doesn't mean she'll want Earth zapped to another dimension,' said Broccoli. He picked up the Two-way Talkie. 'We have to **warn her** about Goospa.'

(He clearly has a **lot** to learn about having a sibling.)

Broccoli flicked the switch to ON. The Two-way Talkie crackled to life. 'Hello,' he said, shouting into it. 'Nishi? It's me, Broccoli! Nishi? Can you hear me?'

The Two-way Talkie sputtered hopelessly.

'The signal's not strong enough,' I said. 'We're too far away. I knew we should have used those quadruple relays!'

'We have to boost the signal,' said Broccoli, frowning. 'There has to be something here we can use—'

'**WOOOOOOOOOEEEEEEEE!**' yelled a voice.

A short distance away from us, Bean was dancing on top of a mound of purple rock. '**WOOEE—AAARRGGGG**H!' A shriek pierced the air as he suddenly fell backwards and dropped down out of sight.

'Bean!' yelled Broccoli. He sprinted towards the rock, Archibald **bouncing** along in his pocket with a disgruntled look on his face. 'I'm coming, Bean!'

I raced after him, sort-of-not-really-hoping that Bean had been eaten so we wouldn't have to worry about him any more.

Panting, we spun round the rock and –
BLOP! BLOP!

Two marshmallows whizzed through the air at *rocket speed*. One hit Broccoli on the nose; the other smacked me on the forehead.

'Ooh – double bullseye,' cackled Bean. 'You should have seen your faces! Scaredy-cats!'

'This isn't a joke, Bean!' said Broccoli crossly. He rubbed his nose, which was already turning strawberry-red. 'Do you have any idea how much **trouble** we're in?'

'I was *about* to ask you the very same,' said a voice behind us.

How I, Nishi Verma,
Detected an Alien Life Form

(told by Nishi Verma, with interruptions from her <u>ANNOYING</u> sister)

Weather: sunny with a light breeze. Sky is
generally clear with some cirrus clouds.

Dear Reader,

Before I begin my account of how I detected an alien life form
in my own home, I would like to introduce myself. My name is Nishi
Verma and I am a meteorologist of the Guild of Junior Meteorologists
(GUM for short). I am sure that you will have heard about me from
Esha. I am also sure that anything she has told you is wrong.

DRONG

Me

[A note from Esha: Nishi, I told you that you can't write like a DRONG in my journal.]

Esha, I am not interested in writing in your journal and I'm only doing it as a favour because you begged me to.

[A note from Esha: I did **NOT**. I also did NOT tell you to begin *your* side of *the story* yet, so you'll just have to wait your turn.]

Rescued (sort of)

I whipped round at the sound of the voice, expecting to find a **PURPLE ROCK CREATURE** behind us.

It wasn't a purple rock creature.

It was a *girl*.

SUPER
COOL
OUTFIT

Her trousers were stitched from a colourful patchwork of cloth. Sparkly stars glittered on her socks and boots. Her blazer was red and made of some sort of shiny fabric with pockets sewn onto the sleeves.

I glanced at my own T-shirt. **Pockets on the sleeves!** That was unbelievably cool (and clever). Why hadn't I thought of that?

'Stay back!' said Bean. He leapt to his feet and slid a marshmallow into his slingshot. 'I warn you – we're armed and *dangerous!*'

Archibald made a noise that sounded like, 'Oh, the embarrassment.'

Broccoli pulled Bean back. 'Will you stop it?' he whispered fiercely.

I was still *staring* at the girl's outfit. It wasn't just cool. It was

SUPER DUPER MARVELLOSO.

I made a note to myself to make a matching blazer as soon as I got home.

The girl looked us up and down in puzzlement. 'Are you Earthlings?' she said. She spoke slowly, **stretching** out each word as if it was a wad of bubblegum.

'How do you know?' said Broccoli.

She wrinkled her nose. 'I can smell it on you,' she said. 'You are far from home.'

'We are? I mean – I know we are,' I said (after all, I couldn't let the girl think I was a total IGNORAMUS). 'We are very far. **Extremely**. Because Earth is Earth and we are here and here is . . . not Earth.'

Broccoli sighed. 'Could you tell us where we are?'

'Planet 403. It is a **NO-GO** planet,' said the girl. 'One of the most dangerous in the entire galaxy. How did you even get here?'

'Did you say **dangerous?**' squeaked Broccoli.

'We came through a portal,' said Bean. 'I told them that's what it was, but **they** didn't believe me.'

'*Bean!*' hissed Broccoli. 'Will you please keep quiet?'

'A portal?' The girl frowned. 'Do you mean a spatial anomaly? Where did that come from? Spatial anomalies do **not** just *appear*.'

'This portal was—' began Bean.

'An accident,' I interrupted quickly before Bean completely destroyed my genius reputation. I cleared my throat. It was time to introduce myself properly. 'My name is Esha Verma and I am a **genius inventor** extraordinaire. This is my apprentice, Broccoli.'

'I'm Bean!' piped up Bean. 'Slingshot supremo—'

'We were in the process of inventing an invisibility device,' I said, 'but it – uh – malfunctioned slightly.'

'*Slightly?*' said the girl. 'To create an anomaly, you would need to build a device that can generate its own **SPATIAL ENERGY,** enough to overcome the existing forces between dimensions and—'

Bean yawned loudly.

She stopped and NARROWED her eyes at him. 'It is near impossible,' she finished. 'How exactly did you manage it?'

'Well we were trialling our invisibility device – and then a hole appeared—'

'And then that slimy Goospa came through,' added Bean unhelpfully. 'He's from Planet Zelpha.'

'Goospa?' said the girl sharply. 'Goospa is on Earth?'

'You know him?' said Broccoli.

The girl scowled. 'Know him? That foul-brained **toad-mushroom** tried to steal my ship. My ship, you understand? He is a – a – crispbread – no . . . What do you Earthlings say? A criminal. I am trying to track him down.'

'BOR-ING,' said Bean. 'Who are YOU anyway?'

'Bean,' hissed Broccoli.

'What?' He stared at the girl expectantly. 'We've told you who we are. Now it's your turn. If this planet is so dangerous, why are *you* here?'

The girl eyed Bean as if he was the **MOST DISGUSTING BUG** she had ever set eyes upon. 'My name is Nix. I am a member of **PADRRU**, the Planetary and Dimensional Rapid Response Unit. We track down crispbreads like Goospa.'

I looked at her in admiration. Nix didn't just have a cool outfit. She also had a cool job.

'We've heard of them,' I said, nodding furiously. 'Isn't that right, Broccoli?'

'Er – well—'

'I haven't,' said Bean. He folded his arms and gave her an unimpressed look. 'Prove it.'

EURGH.

'Sorry about him.' I glared at Bean. 'He doesn't know anything about talking to people.'

'And he doesn't mean to be so rude, do you, Bean?' said Broccoli.

'Actually, I do,' said Bean. 'How do we know you're from this paddy – pad—'

'PADRRU,' said Nix coolly.

'Yeah. That. Show us some ID.'

She sighed. 'Here.' She flashed a shiny badge at us, then slipped it back inside her pocket.

'That was too quick!' protested Bean. 'I didn't even see. Show us again!'

'That won't be necessary,' I said. 'You said that Goospa stole your ship?'

'Yes,' said the girl. 'Goospa snuck onboard and **hijacked** my ship mid-flight. During our struggle, he ejected me! From my own ship! I landed on this planet.' She scowled. 'But that toad-mushroom does not have a smidgen of piloting skill. He ejected himself onto

this planet and let my beautiful ship

CRASH LAND

 on its surface. I have been looking for him
since. And now you say this crispbread is
on Earth? Due to a spatial anomaly *you*
created?'

I flushed. When you put it like *that*, it did not sound
good.

'Where is this anomaly now?'

'Well – it was – uh . . .' I glanced back over my shoulder,
but the rock around us looked the same in all directions.
'Around there,' I estimated, waving to my left. 'But it's
closed now.'

'Closed?' said Nix, frowning. 'Then we need to find him
another way.'

'Is PADRRU linked to The Office of Time?' asked
Broccoli.

'T.O.O.T.? Those ridiculous time tiddlers?' Nix shook her
head. 'No, nada, no. PADRRU is far superior to T.O.O.T.'

'We know Secondus,' I added. 'Secondus Secondi. He's a
Middle Officer of Time at T.O.O.T.'

'How fascinating for him.'

'But **you** can help us, right?' said Broccoli hopefully. 'Secondus did.'

'Well, we helped each other,' I pointed out. 'Our Throat Ticklers are now part of T.O.O.T.'s essential kit for their officers—'

'**BOR-ING,**' said Bean. He stuck his tongue out at Archibald, who made a noise that sounded like, 'You will pay for your insolence, foolish boy-child.'

'Goospa wants to teleport Earth,' continued Broccoli. 'He wants to take it back to Zelpha so his parents can have blueberries or something. He's going to do it today, at 3.30 p.m. – he called it The Optimum Time and he's—'

'**Teleport Earth?**' said Nix incredulously. 'But that is **impossible.** You cannot teleport a planet without a teleportation device.'

'He said he would build one.'

'**Codswallop.** You cannot build a teleportation device without Zirboonium and there is (no) Zirboonium on Earth.' She smirked. 'If Goospa were not a foul-brained toad-mushroom, he would know that.'

'Did you say . . . Zirboonium?' said Broccoli, his snot trembling as he looked at me.

UH OH.

'Yes. But there is no Zirboonium on Earth . . . is there?' said Nix slowly, looking between the two of us. *'Is there?'*

'Well – actually . . .' I took a deep breath; then I told her about the Young Inventor of the Year contest and the **Brain Trophy** being made out of Zirboonium.

Nix listened in silence, her face growing more and *more* **cross** until she looked like a hedgehog that had eaten a pickled onion.

'So – to be clear as custard – you Earthlings found Zirboonium in a meteorite and you made a *trophy* from it?' said Nix, once I had finished.

'Not just any trophy,' I said proudly. '**THE Brain Trophy**. For the best Young Inventor of the Year.'

'Which means Goospa *can* make the teleportation device! We have to save Earth!' said Broccoli. His snot had dropped to **ULTRA-WORRY** mode. 'It's in terrible danger!'

'Not just Earth,' said Nix. 'If Goospa teleports your planet, the **ENTIRE GALAXY** is in

TERRIBLE DANGER.

Spatial teleportation is infinitely complicated. You cannot simply move a planet from one planetary dimension to another. There are too many variables. Get it even slightly wrong and the inter-planetary elliptics will be sloppled, the cosmos co-ordinates **caboodled**.'

'And that's bad?' I said.

'Bad? Goospa could tear the whole galaxy apart.' Her forehead was crinkled with worry. 'He must not locate the Zirboonium by The Optimum Time.'

'The whole galaxy?' whispered Broccoli. 'Oh no. Esha, what have we done?'

'We didn't do anything. This is all Goospa's fault,' I reminded him, hoping Mum and Dad would see it the same way.

'I must find him **before** he builds this device,' said Nix. 'And **YOU** are coming with me.'

'**BOR-ING,**' said Bean. 'Why do we have to go with you?'

'Because you are going to take me to Goospa,' said Nix. 'In exchange, I will get you off this planet.'

'Who said we want to get off this planet?' said Bean. 'I want to explore. I'm going to be the first boy from Earth to—'

Broccoli clapped a hand over Bean's mouth. 'That sounds fair,' he said quickly. 'Isn't that right, Esha? We take Nix to Goospa and she *gets us off this dangerous planet.*' He gave me a pointed SAY YES QUICKLY look.

'Absolutely,' I said. 'Completely and totally fair.' (If we were lucky, maybe we'd be able to find Goospa and fix this unpleasant situation before lunchtime. As for the **Brain Trophy** – well – I'd worry about that *when* we'd saved Earth. After all, there would be no contest at all if the whole galaxy got **destroyed**.)

I stepped forward and held my hand out to Nix. 'It's a deal,' I said.

She stared at me in confusion. 'Why are you showing me your hand?'

'To shake on it,' I said. 'So you know it's a deal.'

'Did you not say so already?'

'Well, yes,' I said, 'but this confirms it.'

'How reassuring,' said Nix. Ignoring my hand, she pulled out a yellow frisbee-shaped disc from her pocket, which she put on the ground in front of us. Crouching down, she pushed a green button on its surface and stepped back.

A second later, the disc shuddered. It **bounced** across the ground like a claw-dancing crab, then, with the softest of clicks, it slid open. I gasped as a complex network of wooden panels and levers unfolded into the air until we were looking at this:

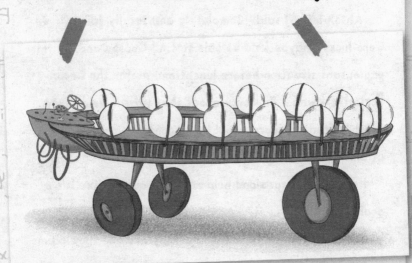

My inventor's instincts itched with

SPINGLY-TINGLY delight.

'What *is* that?' I murmured.

'Planet buggy,' said Nix. 'Suitable for all land terrain.'
She strode forward. 'Move, Earthlings. We cannot get off
this planet until we locate my ship.'

Bean pulled Broccoli's hand away from his mouth and
glared suspiciously at Nix.

'Locate your ship? You don't even know where it is? How
do you know it hasn't been smashed to tiny pieces?'

'Because, Earthling,' said Nix, pausing to give him a
venomous look, 'I activated the emergency shield before
Goospa ejected me. It is still emitting a
signal, which means it is quite safe. I have
the co-ordinates for its location. Any more
useless questions?'

Bean pouted and folded his arms across his chest.

'I thought not,' said Nix, continuing towards the buggy.

'Broccoli, look at it,' I breathed. 'What a *feat of
engineering.*'

'You **really** want to go with her?' said Bean. 'How do

you even know she's who she says she is? She didn't show us her badge properly.'

'Bean, we don't have time for this,' said Broccoli impatiently. 'If we don't get off this planet and find Goospa, he could teleport Earth and destroy the entire galaxy.'

I couldn't take my eyes off the planet buggy. 'Those compression mechanisms are *unbelievably difficult* to get right,' I murmured.

Bean stuck out his chin. 'But I don't want to leave. I want to explore! This is my first time on a different planet and—'

'And nothing,' said Broccoli firmly. 'Aunt Wendy told me to look after you and that's what I'm doing. We're going with Nix whether you like it or not.'

At that moment the buggy spurted to life, the entire contraption rattling and shaking with a loud **THRUM-VHRUM** noise.

Bean's face lit up.

'Woah,' he said. 'Now *that's* cool.'

'**GET A HURRY ON, EARTHLINGS!**' shouted Nix from the buggy walkway.

Bean slid his slingshot into his pocket. 'Race you, bore-brains,' he called, running towards her.

'Bean, wait for us!' shouted Broccoli.

'He really is the **most** irritating seven-year-old on the planet,' I growled as we sprinted after him.

'Make that the entire galaxy!' huffed Broccoli.

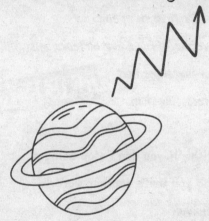

An _Important_ Interruption
from Nishi Verma

(told mostly by Nishi)

Dear Reader,

Finally, Esha has agreed that it makes sense for you to know what was happening back on Earth at this point.

For this reason, I, Nishi Verma, official GUM meteorologist, will be writing this section. I can guarantee that you will find it far more interesting than anything Esha has to say.

GUARANTEE

[A note from Esha: Nishi, if you don't stop being a DRONG, I'm not letting you write another word.]

Let me start at the beginning.

On the morning the portal was opened by my _idiot_ sister, I was busy writing up my weekly weather report. There was a strange anomaly in the atmospheric pressure – which I only later realized must have been caused by Esha's invention opening a portal in the shed.

I was just about to re-examine my readings when I heard a loud SCRITCH–SCRITCH at my door.

Monday

+21°

Tuesday

+18°

'Esha!' I shouted. 'Berty's scratching my door again! Will you take him away? I'm trying to concentrate!'

SCRITCH–SCRITCH.

'ESHA!'

SCRITCH–SCRITCH.

SCRITCH–SCRITCH.

I sighed. Ever since a T-rex had come into my life, I hadn't had a single moment of peace. NOT ONE! Throwing down my pen, I marched across my room and yanked open the door. Berty sprang back quicker than a lightning bolt and looked at me with an angelic expression on his face. I stared at the jagged lines carved into the wood of my door and raised my eyebrows.

'I know that was you, Berty,' I said. 'I have an important weather report to write, so leave me alone.'

He blinked at me, his tail thumping happily against the carpet.

'Esha!' I yelled. 'I've told you not to let this dinosaur wander around the house without supervision. He's a T-rex, for goodness' sake!'

[A note from Esha: Technically speaking, Berty is still not the expected dimensions of a T-rex. I am almost certain this must have **some**thing to do with

93

what happened at the Central Research Laboratory. My investigations are still ongoing.]

Berty blinked at me and stuck his tongue up his nose.

'I thought T-rexes were meant to be smart,' I muttered.

That's when my annoying sister opened her bedroom door.

'Esha!' I glared at her. 'Didn't you hear me calling you? Look at what your silly dinosaur did to my door! Don't think for a second that I'm not telling Mum and Dad. They're going to be furious when they see it!'

Esha blinked at me very, very slowly.

'Mum, Dad,' she said. 'Sister.'

'Did you even hear what I just said?'

'I am sorry, dear sister.'

I stared at her. 'What did you say?'

'I am sorry,' she said again.

I blinked. In all my life, Esha had never apologized to me.

Not once. Not even when she'd STOLEN my tickets to the Central Research Laboratory and ruined my

chances of appearing on TV and becoming an instant METEOROLOGICAL star like my hero Nimbus Dewey.

[A note from Esha: As I've explained to Nishi many times, I didn't steal the tickets. I was only planning to borrow them for a short while.]

'You're sorry?'

'Indeed, dear sister.'

I raised my eyebrows. 'Is this another one of your weird experiments?'

'Experiment? I think not. Har-Har.'

I stared at her, then at Berty, who looked as confused as me. Shuffling forward, he sniffed Esha's feet. Almost at once, he roared and leapt back behind me, his entire body quivering.

'Berty? What's got into you?' I said. 'It's Esha, you silly dinosaur!'

'Esha?' called Mum from downstairs. 'Are you back from Broccoli's? Did you get your homework done?'

'Home-work?' said Esha slowly. 'Yes. Home-work is complete.'

'I'm going to the supermarket. Either of you want to come?'

'The super-market?' Esha's face lit up. 'I know about the super-market. Har-Har. The core of Earthly supplies. Including the blue-berry.'

[A note from Esha: I have since pointed out to Nishi that if she had even half a brain, she would have realized I was not MYSELF.]

(And I have told Esha that it's not the first time
she's behaved weirdly. In fact, most of
the words that come out of her mouth
make as much sense as snow in the Sahara.)

'Yes, Mother,' said Esha. 'I would love to accompany you to the super-market.'

Mother?

If Esha thought that being polite to Mum would stop her from being banned from inventing, she was even less of a genius than she thought.

'But you hate going to the supermarket,' I said.
'Last week you said you'd rather have all your teeth pulled out than waste your genius time shopping for onions.'

'I am not that person now,' said Esha. 'No, I am not. Har-Har.'

'Whatever.' I leaned over the banister. 'I'll come too, Mum.'
Berty was still quivering against my legs. 'This month's GUM topic is wind resistance. I need to get a few things for my latest investigation.'

'Wind resistance,' said Esha. She smiled. 'Fascinating, Har-Har.'

I stared at her.

Esha had never called my weather investigations fascinating.
Boring – many times. Dreary – definitely. Fascinating – never.

And there was something about her smile that sent an Arctic-level shiver down my spine.

'I know what you're playing at,' I hissed, taking a step towards her. 'You think you can be nice to me and I'll forgive you for what happened at the Central Research Laboratory. Well, I won't. You stole my chance to become a TV star!'

Esha blinked at me.

'Come on, you two!' called Mum. 'I'm leaving now.'

'Time to leave, Har-Har,' said Esha. 'For the super-market.' She glanced warily at Berty, then turned towards the stairs.

Berty whined and pressed his face against my leg.

'Eurgh!' I said as a blob of dinosaur drool dribbled down my trousers. 'Can't you be careful, Berty?'

He whined again.

'Don't think I don't know your tricks. I'm still telling Mum and Dad that you scratched my door.'

'Shall we proceed to the core of Earthly supplies, Mother?' echoed Esha's voice from downstairs. 'I would like to get some Zir—'

With a frightened roar, Berty bolted into my room.

I sighed. Sometimes, I wasn't sure what was worse. Living with Esha or a T-rex.

Why a No-Go Planet Is a No-Go Planet

'Onwards!' said Nix, hopping in front of a console as we followed Bean onto the open deck. There was a loud

CLUNK as she pulled a red lever. A moment later, the buggy zipped forward with a **loud THRUM-VHRUM-THRUM**.

The landscape sped by in a purple *blur.*

Bean whooped loudly and ran towards the back of the buggy.

'Bean, don't get too near the edge!' shouted Broccoli. Archibald rolled his eyes and made a noise that sounded like, 'Push the worm overboard.'

I peered over the side, full of inventor's admiration at such a contraption. The wheels chugged along the rocky ground at breathtaking speed, their loud **THRUM-VHRUM-THRUM** rattling my insides. A warm wind whipped past my face, the bitter smell of the planet making my nostrils curl. In the distance, scattered between the rocks, I spotted a cluster of knobbly grey stumps rising out of the ground.

I turned around to Nix, who was bent over the console. 'What are those?' I asked.

'You Earthlings would call them trees,' she said, following my hand.

'Those are trees?' I said. 'But they look so shrivelled.'

'It is a No-Go planet,' Nix said. 'Those shrivelled stumps are stronger than you feeble Earthlings.' She traced a ZIG ZAG PATH on the screen with her finger.

'This should be the quickest route to my ship,' she murmured.

'Feeble Earthlings?' I said incredulously. 'I've travelled through all of time and space already.'

Nix grunted.

'I've escaped a Guzzler, too.' I paused, waiting for this piece of information to sink in.

Still nothing. Not even a flicker to show she was a teensy-tiny bit impressed.

'Did I mention that I'm a **genius inventor**? I can show you some of my inventions, if you like. Maybe there'll be something here that PADRRU can use.' I stuck my hand into my Inventor's Kit. 'I have the fifth prototype of the Boomers – the **ULTIMATE** *noise-creation* devices – and the—'

'CHECK OUT OUR SPEED!' shouted Bean.

'THIS IS AWESOME!'

A few marshmallows whizzed through the air in different directions. One **bounced** off Nix's head with a BLOP! and disappeared over the edge of the buggy. Nix went rigid, then slowly turned and shot Bean a look of disgust.

'I'm extremely sorry about that,' said Broccoli. The tips of his ears had turned scarlet. 'Bean is – uh – well, Bean. He's *excited*. He's never been on a new planet before.'

Nix looked Broccoli up and down. 'Are you his brother, Earthling?'

'No,' said Broccoli. 'I'm his cousin.'

'How lucky for you,' said Nix. She turned back to the screen. 'Brothers – **BLURGH**.

Silly, interfering, chit-chattering **NOISE BALLS**. Nothing more, nothing less.'

'That's what I always say,' I said, nodding furiously. 'I've got a sister. Nishi. She's a total DRONG.'

'**WAAAHOOOOO!**' yelled Bean.

I turned around – but Bean wasn't there.

He'd disappeared overboard.

(Thank goodness.)

Well, that's what I thought at first. He had, in fact, hooked his legs onto the deck's rail and was **dangling** upside down from the buggy.

'Can it go any faster?'

'**BEAN!**' shrieked Broccoli. He sped forward and wrestled him back onto the deck. 'Are you out of your mind? What do you think you're doing?'

'Having FUN!' retorted Bean.

'F-U-N.

FUN.

Oh, wait. I forgot. You don't know the meaning of that word. We're on a whole other planet. We should explore what's out there. Who knows what we'll find?'

'Or what will find you,' said Nix.

Bean blinked. 'I'm not scared,' he said, though he suddenly sounded a little less sure of himself. He waved his slingshot at her. 'I can look after myself.'

'You really are a silly Earthling,' Nix said. 'Do you know why Planet 403 is a No-Go planet? What makes it so dangerous?'

  Bean stuck out his chin. 'Haven't seen anything dangerous.'

'Yet,' said Nix. 'Planet 403 is one of the most *unfriendly* planets in the entire galaxy. As darkness falls, the temperature will drop. There are few sources of food or water. Lava marshes. Ice Bats.' She paused, her face paling a little. 'And there is . . . worse. *Much worse.*'

'Worse?' mumbled Broccoli.

'A creature you should hope we **do not** encounter.'

She pressed a few buttons on her screen. With a loud crackle, a shimmering projection shot into the air above our heads.

'See this, Earthling? This is the PLANET SAFETY SCALE.'

I breathed in sharply.

The scale was beautiful.

[A note from Broccoli: BEAUTIFUL was NOT my first thought. Terrifying, maybe.]

The scale was shaped like a long, twisting coil, which shone with countless miniaturized planets and stars. Nix jabbed a finger to the far end, where a handful of teensy-tiny planets floated in the air. 'Do you see the colour of the scale here? Red. Red for extreme danger, because these are No-Go planets.' She pointed to one at the furthest end. 'This one here is Planet 403. One of the **most dangerous.**

You **DO NOT** land on such planets.
No, nada, no. You **DO NOT** travel across
them. No, nada, no. And you **DO NOT**
get stranded on them. No, nada, **NO.'** She jabbed a
button and the scale disappeared with an angry crackle.
'Understand, Earthling?'

Bean slid his slingshot into his pocket and folded his
arms across his chest. 'I'm still not scared.'

Archibald gave him an irritated look. It was the most
irritated look I had ever seen on the face of a tortoise.

Broccoli rubbed a hand through his hair. He looked even
more **frazzled** than the time Archibald had disappeared
at the park (what else did he expect,
putting a tortoise down in grass? It took
us HOURS to find him).

'Listen,' Broccoli said. 'We need to try and contact Earth.'

'There are no communication devices on this buggy,
Earthling,' said Nix, eyes on the console.

Broccoli took out the Two-way Talkie. 'I have
this talkie—'

'Taw-kie?' said Nix, looking at it in
puzzlement.

'It's – uh – a communication device, but the signal's not strong enough. Can you help boost it?'

'You wish to strengthen the signal of your communication device?'

'Exactly,' said Broccoli.

Nix eyed the device, then she pointed to a hexagonal panel at the edge of the console. 'That is an extrapolator. I believe that is what you require to strengthen the signal of your **taw-kie.**'

Broccoli's face lit up. 'Can I use it?'

'Use it?' Nix snorted. 'No, **nada, no,** Earthling! Do you want us to reach my ship? Using the extrapolator will risk draining the buggy's energy supplies. This thing doesn't run on – on . . . What do you call it?' She clicked her fingers impatiently. 'Ants, apples – air!

It does not run on air, Earthling! Your message will have to wait.'

'But it's important,' said Broccoli with a sniff. 'We have to warn Esha's sister that the Esha on Earth isn't Esha. Goospa **shapeshifted** into her.'

Nix stared at him. 'Repeat yourself, Earthling.'

'Goospa **shapeshifted** into Esha.'

'That toad-mushroom,' muttered Nix. 'He has been trouble from the moment—' She cleared her throat. 'You have my word that he will face the strictest punishment.'

'What about the message?' asked Broccoli.

'You can send it when we reach my ship. Until then, you wait, Earthling.'

Broccoli glanced at me, looking worried. I shrugged. I was in no rush to contact Earth. Just the thought of Nishi finding out about Goospa made me want to PUKE.

Broccoli's eyes lingered on the console, then he slipped the Two-way Talkie into his pocket.

'Fine. I'll wait, then.'

[A note from Broccoli: Chapter 66 of the *Inventor's Handbook* says that *the best inventors wait for the right time to strike. This is called The Golden Moment.*]

The buggy rocked *wildly* as we danced forward. For miles around all we could see was an **ENORMOUS stretch** of purple rock and . . . more purple rock. The ground was *rough* and **bumpy**, like a ⓖⓘⓐⓝⓣ ⓒⓗⓔⓔⓢⓔ ⓖⓡⓐⓣⓔⓡ. Above us, the sky shimmered softly, green and silver light swirling between the pink.

We hadn't been travelling for long when, in the distance, I spotted faint plumes of smoke spiralling up from the ground and disappearing into the air.

'Lava marshes,' said Nix grimly. 'We stay clear of those or we will be **melted, softened, liquefied**. Like – like . . . What do you call it?

Welly! You'll become welly!'

'Do you mean jelly?' said Broccoli.

'Jelly-welly-welly-jelly,' said Nix, waving a hand.

'Bor-ing,' said Bean, who was polishing his slingshot.

'How long have you been at PADRRU?' I asked. 'It sounds like a cool job.'

Nix squinted into the distance, her face darkening. 'Curse of The Free Moons,' she muttered. She jabbed a few buttons on the console. With a loud **sputter**, the buggy came to a sudden **STOP.** ←

'What is it?' said Broccoli. 'Why are we stopping?'

Nix twisted a couple of tiny wheels. A moment later, a sparkly haze of purple swept across the buggy around us.

'What is that?' murmured Bean. He reached up to touch the light with his fingers.

'No touching, Earthling,' snapped Nix, slapping his hand away. 'Camouflage shields are highly sensitive.'

'Camouflage shield?' My eyes widened as I stared at the glittering light around us. 'We're camouflaged?'

'Why do we need camouflage?' said Broccoli.

'For that, Earthling,' said Nix, pointing. In the distance ahead of us, a silvery-blue glint was sweeping across the sky in our direction. It looked like a COLOSSAL, angry storm cloud. Only as it moved closer I realized it wasn't a storm cloud at all.

It was, in fact, a cluster of flying creatures.

The most peculiar flying creatures I had EVER SEEN.

They looked about the same size as an eagle, and their bodies were long and *stringy* like rubber bands. Their skin was speckled with silver spots. Each creature had gleaming talons and two pairs of **ENORMOUS** wings, which glistened like the finest spider silk. All I could see of their faces was a pair of RAZOR-SHARP fangs, which glistened menacingly against the sky.

'Pterodactyls,' breathed Bean.

Broccoli sighed. 'Don't be ridiculous, Bean. Those aren't pterodactyls.'

'How do you know?'

'Because their heads are the wrong shape and—'

'Quiet, Earthlings!' said Nix, glaring at them. 'Those are **Ice Bats.** They will *ice-cream you*, understand? Freeze your ins-and-outs, then slurp up all the juice.'

'Juice?' echoed Broccoli, his snot quivering.

The Ice Bats were only a short distance away now, close enough for us to hear their ear-piercing *shrieks* as they called to one another.

SQUAAAA! SQUAAAA!
SQUAAAA! SQUAAAA!

'You don't need to be afraid, Bean,'
said Broccoli (even though he looked the <u>**MOST**</u>
terrified out of all of us).

[A note from Broccoli: I did not.]

'I won't let anything happen to you.'

Archibald blinked at Broccoli and snickered
as if to say, 'What about me?'

'Afraid? I'm not afraid,' said Bean. He
waved his slingshot at him. 'I can take them.'

'Shhh,' hissed Nix as the Ice Bats approached. 'We have
the camouflage shield. If we are ducky, they will not spot us.'

'Do you mean lucky?' I suggested helpfully.

SQUAAAA! SQUAAAA!

The Ice Bats flew with ferocious speed,
their wings swishing loudly across the air.
I watched, spellbound,
as they approached, the shield hiding us from view.

'You're all *so* boring,' said Bean with a sigh. He pointed at me then at Broccoli. '**BOR-ING, more BOR-ING.**' He stuck his tongue out at Archibald, who gave him a villainous glare in return. '**Most BOR-ING.**'

'Be quiet, Bean,' whispered Broccoli fiercely.

For one merciful moment there was silence.

'Pull string to activate,' murmured Bean. '**Interesting.**'

I turned. My eyes widened as I spotted the circular object in his hands.

I knew exactly what that was.

A B**OOM**Er.

'Bean,' hissed Broccoli. 'Where did you get that? Put it down right—'

Bean wasn't listening. Instead, he did the **ONE THING** that he should not have done at that *particular* moment.

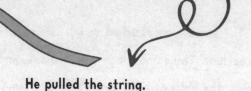

He pulled the string.

Caramelizer Lollies

'No!' I hissed.

'No!' whispered Broccoli.

For a teensy-tiny second, nothing happened.

Bean opened his mouth. **'BOR—'**

BOOM-CRASH-WALLOP-BOOM-BOOM-CRASH-WALLOP-

→ BOOM-

The Boomer **exploded** to life, its noise echoing in all directions. The camouflage shield shook, once, twice, three times, the balls of light **trembling** around us.

'Bean!' hissed Broccoli as the Ice Bats suddenly swivelled their heads towards the sound. 'I told you not to—'

SQUAAAAAAAA!

With a heart-dropping, **toe-curling** shriek, the first Ice Bat opened its mouth and fired a jagged bolt of black ice towards us. (UH OH.)

'They have seen us!' shouted Nix, her fingers dancing across the console with electric speed. 'Your sound-globe compromised the shield – Jinx of The Jabbering Jupiters, we have to **move!**'

THRUM-VHRUM-THRUM!

The buggy **roared** forward, the bolt of ice missing us by a hair's width as we shot across the ground. The camouflage shield **danced** above our heads, the light flickering between different shades of purple – from amethyst to coral to grape to lavender.

'What's happening?' squealed Broccoli, clinging onto the side of the buggy.

'It cannot hold!' yelled Nix. 'We are moving too fast, Earthlings! Camouflage shields are not designed for tweed!'

'Do you mean speed?' I shouted.

The shield crackled, before disappearing with a sorry **sputter**.

We were suddenly **VERY** visible.

SQUAA! SQUAA!

The Ice Bats dived towards us, their faces twisted in vicious delight.

'Can we fix the shield?' I shouted, my teeth **rattling** as we bounced forward. 'I'm sure I can!'

'No, nada, **no!**' bellowed Nix. 'You cannot, Earthling!'

'THIS IS BRILLIANT!' shouted Bean.

Another corkscrew of ice whizzed down and pierced the ground behind us.

BOOM-CRASH-WALLOP-BOOM-BOOM-CRASH-WALLOP-BOOM –

'Can't you fight them off?' bellowed Broccoli.

'This is a transportation vehicle!' retorted Nix. 'It is not designed for fighting Ice Bats!'

'Leave this to me!' said Bean. Slotting the Boomer into his slingshot, he darted towards the back of the buggy. 'Eat this, Snow-Breath!' he shouted, aiming it upwards.

'No, Bean!' shouted Broccoli. '**Don't–**'

BOOM-CRASH-WALLOP-BOOM-BOOM-CRASH-WALLOP-BOOM -

Bean released the Boomer. It sailed through the air, uP and UP, and BOPPED the first Ice Bat directly on its pancake-shaped nose.

'Got you!' hollered Bean in delight. 'Did you see that? That's what you call a bullseye shot!'

'Now you've done it,' whispered Broccoli, his eyes fixed upwards.

SQUAAAA! SQUAAAA!

The Ice Bats were changing position, lining up alongside one another to form an arrowhead formation.

'You think that's going to scare me?' yelled Bean. 'I'm not scared! I'm not—'

SQUAAAA! SQUAAAA!

The Ice Bats opened their mouths.

A MAELSTROM of ice torpedoed down towards us.

'NOT GOOD,' shouted Nix. 'NO, NADA, NO!'

The buggy swerved and zigzagged across the ground as she tried to dodge the icy bolts. I flew sideways and crashed into Broccoli, the two of us sliding across to the edge of the buggy.

'IS THAT THE BEST YOU'VE GOT?' bellowed Bean.

(I wished he'd stop talking.)

One after another, the ice corkscrews **SMASHED** into the ground, forming a polar plateau behind us. The bats loomed closer, their large, transparent wings swishing through the air. They were close enough now for us to see their faces — cold, hungry, with mouths full of **FANGS**.

'Uh – Nix?' said Broccoli, staggering to his feet. 'Can't you go any faster?'

'We are at maximum speed already!' shouted Nix. 'This is a buggy, not a Loonis ship!'

'What's a **Loonis ship?**' asked Broccoli.

'DOES THAT MATTER?' I shouted, as another burst of black ice blasted towards us.

'COME ON THEN!' shouted Bean, his face bright with excitement. He climbed onto the back rail of the buggy, his slingshot held up to the sky.

'YOU **CAN'T** DEFEAT THE SLINGSHOT SUPREMO!'

'BEAN!' shrieked Broccoli. 'GET DOWN FROM THERE!'

A missile of ice blasted towards the buggy, narrowly missing the tail end. It veered unsteadily, the wheels **bouncing** *dangerously* across the rock.

'YOU MISSED!' hollered Bean, wobbling to and fro. 'DID YOU HEAR ME, FROST-FACE. YOU **MISSED**!'

'He's going to hurt himself,' said Broccoli. He pushed Archibald into my hands. 'Hold Archie. I have to get him.'

Archibald snickered in outrage, a sound that seemed to say, 'You think that brain-of-earwig is more important than me?'

'Bean, get back!' shouted Broccoli, skidding across the deck. 'This is no time for heroics!'

'Actually, this is the perfect time for heroics,' I murmured. If I could stop the Ice Bats, Nix would see that I wasn't a feeble Earthling. This was the moment to stun her with my GENIUS.

Keeping hold of Archibald, I scrabbled in my Inventor's Kit until I found what I was looking for.

'Caramelizer Lollies,' I said, pulling out a shiny green case, which had a huge label that said NOT FOR EATING. 'Designed to slow down DRONGS, arch-nemeses and T-REXES. Wait and watch, Archibald – *these* should do the trick!'

But Archibald wasn't listening to me. Instead, he was staring at Broccoli, who was still trying to wrestle Bean off the back of the buggy. If I hadn't known that evil tortoise better, I would have thought he looked – almost – well – JEALOUS.

'There!' shouted Nix, pointing to a thick forest of knobbly grey stumps ahead of us. 'We can take cover there!'

Unfortunately, the Ice Bats seemed to have seen it too. They began firing even faster, ice whizzing around us with ferocious speed.

SQUAA! SQUAA!

SQUAAAA! SQUAAAA!

Another round of ice rockets pelted towards us, the buggy only just inching ahead. If we were going to make it, I had to move fast—

'I have an idea!' I shouted. I flipped

open the case, plucked out a Caramelizer Lolly and waved it in the air. 'We can use this to slow them down!'

I paused, waiting for someone to congratulate me on my **genius**, but Nix was focused on driving the buggy, and Broccoli and Bean were too busy scrabbling around on the deck to notice.

'OI!' I bellowed at the top of my voice. I waved a lolly at Broccoli's cousin. 'Bean, can you sling one of these?'

Bean pulled himself away from Broccoli and stared at me in total and utter delight. 'Did you just ask me to sling something? Because I can sling **ANYTHING.**'

'Then do it. This is a Caramelizer Lolly.' I pulled out the lollipop safety stick and handed him the solid caramel sphere. 'You have five seconds before it **activates.**'

Bean smirked at Broccoli. 'Watch this, **bore-brain.**'

He spun round and aimed the slingshot at the bats. With **PINPOINT ACCURACY,** he fired the caramel into the sky. It sailed through the air in an eye-wateringly glorious swoop, higher and higher, until it was only a few wingbeats away from the bats.

'It's not doing anything!' shouted Bean. 'Why do <u>none</u> of your inventions—'

POP!

A luminous **bubble** of caramel chewiness exploded

into the air. With a shriek, the first bat flew straight into

it.

'No way,'

whispered Bean.

The bat blinked down at us, confused. The others drew

to a stunned halt, neither of them moving as the first bat

hovered where it was, stuck in a **delightfully sticky**

caramel trap.

'YES!' I punched the air with delight. 'It worked!' I spun round towards the console. 'Nix, did you see—'

'Almost there!' shouted Nix, who had her back to us. I scowled. She had missed the whole thing.

SQUAA! SQUAA!

'Give me another one!' shouted Bean, as the bats sprang back to life. He snatched the case out of my hands, pulled out a second lolly and yanked out the safety stick.

PING!

The second ball of caramel shot through the air and . . . POP! It caught another Ice Bat, enveloping it in a bubble of golden beauty.

SQUAAAA! SQUAAAA!

The other Ice Bats torpedoed towards it, their fangs outstretched.

BOING! BOING! BOING!

They **bounced** right back again, smacking into the bubble so hard that it floated away with the second bat still inside.

'That's caramel brilliance for you!' I shouted in glee.

'Broccoli, you were right to use the extra corn syrup! Nix, you *really* have to see this!'

'I am busy, Earthling!' she bellowed, facing ahead.

'Take that!' shouted Bean, firing another Caramelizer into the sky.

Only this time the Ice Bat at the front was ready for it.

With jaw-dropping elegance, it

c a r t w h e e l e d

through the air and shot a missile of ice at the Caramelizer, which began to curve back down.

TOWARDS US.

'TAKE COVER!' bellowed Broccoli, throwing himself at Bean. The Caramelizer landed on the console with a heart-stopping rattle-tattle.

'Nix!' I shouted, sprinting towards her. 'Get back—'

With a **rapturous belch**, the Caramelizer **BUBBLED**
outwards with such force that Nix was flung across the buggy.

'Nix!' I cried as she crashed onto the deck. 'Are you—'

'Get away from me, Earthling!' She slapped my hand
away and leapt to her feet. Her eyes widened as she
caught sight of the console. The whole thing was enveloped
in a translucent globule of **sticky sweetness**.

'No, **nada, no,**' she breathed. She whipped
back towards us, her eyes glistening with fury.
'Remove this substance, Earthlings!'

'Uh – I – I . . .' I mumbled.

'We can't!' said Broccoli. 'They're **self-
dissolvable.**'

'Self – explain yourself, Earthling!' said Nix.

'It'll dissolve itself after some time,' I said,
trying not to meet her eye.

'**Some time?**' screeched Nix.

'We do not have some time!'

The buggy **twisted** uncontrollably across the rock, swerving away from the grey stumps ahead of us.

SQUAAAA! SQUAAAA!

The Ice Bats were getting closer.

'LOOK!' shouted Broccoli.

He pointed forward, his face paling.

Ahead of us was . . . nothing.

Just a purple cliff edge.

My mouth fell open.

Things had just gone from **BAD** to

EXTREMELY TERRIBLE.

SQUAAAA! SQUAAAA!

'**We're going over!**' shouted Broccoli. 'Esha, hold on to Archie!'

SQUAAAA! SQUAAAA!

Grabbing Bean, he slid across the buggy, looping his arm through the rail. I leapt onto the other side, my arm almost jerking out of its socket as I wrapped myself around the edge like a crab. Nix did the same.

'Get off me, **bore-brain!**' protested Bean. 'I don't need you to—'

But I didn't hear the rest because *at that moment*

the buggy FLEW

over the

EDGE of the CLIFF . . .

into the AIR . . .

then

THUD!

We hit the ground.

DOWN we went –

DOWN –

DOWN –

down the slope.

My fingers and toes **rattled** –

faster and *faster* –

the **SQUAA! SQUAA!** of the Ice Bats

piercing

the sky above us –

the whole buggy **SHAKING**-

and I was (quite sure) we were about to be **iced**

or **crushed** -

when, with a loud

 **SCREECH** -

the buggy **skidded**

to a

HALT.

A <u>Slight</u> Delay

'**GET. OFF. ME!**' Bean untangled himself from Broccoli
and leapt to his feet. His face scrunched up with
confusion. 'Where are the Ice Bats?' he said.
'I can't see a thing.'

Cautiously, I unhooked my arm from the
rail. A **THICK MIST** swirled around us,
pale yellow spirals twisting through the air like
crooked fingers. I could still hear the Ice Bats,
but they sounded fainter.

SQUAA! SQUAA!

SQUAA! SQUAA!

'Sounds like they're moving away,' I said.
I squinted upwards, but it was impossible to see
anything through the mist. 'I don't think they can see us.'

Broccoli sniffed, his snot moving up a centimetre.
'We're saved.' He took Archibald from me and
held him into the air. 'We're saved, Archie!'

128

Archibald glared at him for a long moment, then he slid back into his shell, as if he was sulking.

[A note from Broccoli: He was not sulking. He was just tired.]

Nix untangled herself from the ship's railings.

'PLAGUE-OF-THE-SOLAR-WINDS!'

'Nix, I'm sorry about—' I began.

'Silence, Earthling. It is true what they say about your species. Not a breath of intelligence between you.'

I flushed and looked down at my shoes.

So much for stunning her with my genius.

'Did you see me?' said Bean. His face was glowing with excitement. He held his slingshot into the air as if it was a sceptre and strutted around us. 'The slingshot supremo strikes again! You bore-brains are lucky I was here to save the day—'

'Lucky?' spluttered Broccoli, who looked like he'd been dragged sideways through a hedge and back again. 'Lucky? It's your fault we were attacked in the first place, Bean! Where did you find that Boomer?'

'Boomer? Oh, you mean that noise thing.' Bean shrugged. 'Under your bed.'

Broccoli blinked at him like a stunned fish. 'You – you – you **STOLE** it!' he squeaked. 'You can't just take things that don't belong to you.'

(Told you – he still has **LOTS** to learn about becoming a brother.)

'I didn't see your name on it,' said Bean. 'And if it was so dangerous, you shouldn't have left it lying around for *anyone* to find. Technically speaking, it's *your* fault we were attacked.'

Broccoli's face had turned a *dangerous* shade of raspberry. 'You – I – my fault? This isn't my fault!'

'How long must we wait to be free from this – this – thing?' interrupted Nix, pointing at the caramel bubble.

'It'll dissolve in ten minutes,' I said. 'More or less.'

'More or less?' echoed Nix. 'The Optimum Time fast approaches and we are being delayed by this – this—'

Before she could finish speaking, a low hissing noise ripped through the air. The back of the buggy dipped slightly. Her eyes widened. Without a word, she climbed onto the edge of the ship and leapt overboard.

'KAPUT!' shouted Nix through the mist.
'Plunkered! Scuppered!'

'Uh – Nix?' I peered over the edge, but it was impossible to see anything. 'What's wrong?'

'I have discovered a pumpkin on the wheel.'

'Pumpkin?' said Broccoli in bewilderment.

'I think she means a *puncture,*'

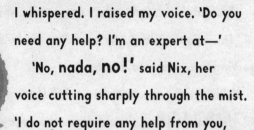

I whispered. I raised my voice. 'Do you need any help? I'm an expert at—'

'No, nada, no!' said Nix, her voice cutting sharply through the mist.

'I do not require any help from you, Earthling. I have exactly what I need. Remain on the buggy.'

'Bor-ing,' said Bean.

'Oh, put a sock in it,' I said.

'*You* put a sock in it,' said Bean. He moved to the back of the buggy and leaned over the edge. 'I want to see what's down there.'

I glared at him. 'Broccoli, can you control your annoying pimple of a—'

BLUB - BLUB -

I turned around as the caramel bubble trembled and BURST, splattering the ship in sweetness. Broccoli ducked. I wiped a blob off my face and smiled. 'Well, that was quicker than I expected. I'll let Nix know.'

'No – wait!' said Broccoli.

He moved towards the console, the Two-way Talkie in his hand.

'Broccoli,' I hissed. 'What are you doing?'

'This is our chance,' he said. 'While she's distracted, I'm getting a message to Earth.'

'Didn't you hear what Nix said? If we plug it into the EXTRAPOLATOR, we could drain the buggy's energy supply. We might never get home. It's **too dangerous.**'

'What's dangerous is not telling anyone on Earth about Goospa. Or have you forgotten there's a shapeshifting alien that looks like you in your shed?' Snot flew into the air as he spoke. 'We have

 to **warn** them. We can't wait until we reach the ship.'

I sighed.

I suppose he sort-of-maybe had a point. But the truth was that the other talkie was with my DRONG of a sister and I *really* didn't want to tell her that I'd accidentally brought a shapeshifting alien from the planet Zelpha onto Earth. Especially when I was **banned** from ınventing.

'Nix said not to.' I pouted.

Broccoli was looking at me as if I was talking gobbledygook.

'Esha, since when do YOU listen to instructions? And have you forgotten Chapter 59 of the *Inventor's Handbook*? A genius inventor should remember that instructions—'

'—are only guidelines and should be treated with *extreme caution*,' I finished. I glanced towards the edge of the buggy. 'Fine – as long as Nix doesn't find out.' The last thing I wanted was for her to think I was an even bigger **IGNORAMUS** than she already did.

'Keep an eye out,' said Broccoli. He placed the Two-way Talkie onto the hexagonal panel, which flashed green and whirred loudly.

'Hello?' said Broccoli, pressing the TALK button. 'Nishi? Can you hear me? It's Broccoli? Hello?'

For a heart-dropping moment there was silence.

'Maybe it's not working,' I said, trying not to sound relieved. 'Or maybe she's not there. She's probably outside cloud-spotting—'

'Hello?' said Nishi's voice.

Ah.

'Er – Nishi? Hello?'

'Broccoli? Is that you? I didn't even think this thing **worked**. What do you want? Be quick, I'm in the middle of writing my weather report.'

'Go on,' he said, looking at me.

'What do you want me to say?' I hissed.

'The truth,' he said. 'She needs to know about Goospa.'

'I already told you. She's not going to believe me.'

'Esha?' Nishi sounded confused. 'Is that you? I thought you were in your room.'

'My room?' My heart skipped a beat. 'Have you . . . seen me in my room?'

'You disappeared inside with a bowl of blueberries after we came back from the supermarket.' She paused. 'I thought you hated blueberries!'

'I went to the supermarket?' I echoed.

Broccoli's eyes were wide.

Nishi sighed impatiently. 'Honestly, Esha, I don't know what games you're playing, but I really don't have time for—'

'Nishi, wait! You have to listen to me. That's not me in my room. That's an **ALIEN** from the planet Zelpha!'

'What?'

'An **ALIEN** from the planet Zelpha!'

'Zelpha? I've never heard of it.'

EURGH.

'Just because you haven't heard of it, doesn't mean it **doesn't exist!** He's planning to teleport Earth to a different dimension. You have to ⓌⒶⓇⓃ ⓣⓗⒺ ⓖⓞⓥⒺⓇⓃⓜⒺⓝⓣ! NASA! Mum and Dad – actually wait, don't tell Mum and Dad.'

'Esha, are you being funny?' snapped my DRONG of a sister.

'Funny? No! I'm completely serious. It's a long story and I don't have time to go into details, but you have to believe me. That alien found his way to Earth, er, somehow and made himself look like me. He's planning to build a teleportation device so he can **STEAL** Earth and he sent us to Planet 403 so we wouldn't get in his way and now we're kind of stuck!'

'Oh, you're trapped on a far-off planet?' interrupted Nishi dryly. 'Isn't that a shame?'

'Nishi, are you even listening to what I'm saying? If he teleports Earth, then the

entire galaxy is in DANGER! You have to—'

'You listen to me, Esha Verma. I don't *have* to do anything. Especially not after you stole my tickets to the Central Research Laboratory AND my chance to appear on TV.'

DOUBLE EURGH.

Not this *again*.

'You haven't even said sorry! Instead you waste my precious time with your stupid jokes. *The entire galaxy is in danger,*' she said, **RUDELY** mimicking me. 'Do you really think I'm that dumb? And – Berty! What are you doing?

Get out of here, you silly dinosaur! Berty! Oh, now look what you've done—' Suddenly her voice was cut off by a **LOUD** crackling.

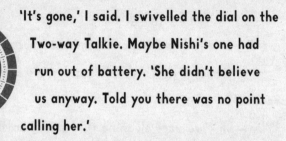

'Nishi?' I said. 'Nishi, can you hear me? This isn't a joke! Nishi!'

But all I could hear was *more* crackling.

'It's gone,' I said. I swivelled the dial on the Two-way Talkie. Maybe Nishi's one had run out of battery. 'She didn't believe us anyway. Told you there was no point calling her.'

'I can't believe she hasn't realized that you're not Goospa!' Broccoli said. 'She's your sister!'

'She's also the biggest DRONG in the entire world,' I reminded him. 'This is what happens when you have your head in the clouds all the time. Trust me, Broccoli. Nishi can't help us. We have to fix this ourselves.'

'I told you to **remain** on the ship!' **thundered** Nix's voice through the air.

Broccoli swept the Two-way Talkie back into his pocket; a second later, Nix climbed back onto the buggy, Bean close behind her. Both of them looked damp from the mist.

'**Bean?**' said Broccoli. 'What were you doing down there? I thought you were **on** the buggy.'

'The Earthling is a nuisance,' said Nix, picking a marshmallow out of her hair. Her eyes NARROWED. 'What are you doing with the console?'

'Oh – uh – we were cleaning it,' I said. I brushed away some stray slivers of caramel and forced a smile onto my face. 'See?'

'I did not ask you to clean it,' said Nix coldly.

'Just being helpful,' I said.

'I do not require **help.**' She pushed past us and began punching co-ordinates into the console. 'The wheel is fixed, but we have gone off-course. We will require a new route to reach the ship.'

'You were supposed to stay here,' hissed Broccoli, glaring at Bean.

Bean rolled his eyes. 'Keep your snot in. I was just having a look. Not that I could see anything. There's too much mist.'

'You can't just **leave** the buggy! What if something had happened to you?'

Bean made a face. 'How many times do I have to tell you? I can look after myself.'

He stuck his tongue out at Archibald.

'I'm not a stupid tortoise.'

Archibald NARROWED his eyes and made a noise that sounded like, 'Perhaps I should throw you overboard myself.'

[A note from Broccoli: Archibald would never say such a thing. As you, the Reader, will know by now, he is an extremely kind and noble creature.]

'Super stars!' shouted Nix. 'We have a new route!'

She pushed a couple of buttons and spun a dial. The spheres around us sparked into life, throwing a bright orange light into the mist. I held my breath as she jabbed the console, hoping we hadn't drained the battery too much.

If the buggy didn't run . . .

VHRUM-THRUM-VHRUM!

I breathed out **in relief** as we leapt forward. Talking to Nishi might have been an **EPIC failure,** but at least the buggy was *moving.* And we'd escaped the Ice Bats. All we had to do now was <u>find</u> Nix's ship, <u>return to Earth</u> and stop Goospa before The Optimum Time.

Easy-peasy.

[A note from Broccoli: That's not how I would have described it.]

Something <u>Unexpected</u>

BLOP!

A marshmallow hit my arm.

BLOP! BLOP!

A couple more **bounced** off the edge of the buggy.

'Bean, will you give it a rest?' I said crossly.

'**BOR-ED,**' he said. The mist twisted around us in thick swirls. 'When are we getting **out** of this mist?'

'We get out when we get out, Earthling.' Nix *bristled.*

'How far are we from the ship?' asked Broccoli.

'Far enough,' she grunted.

'We've been driving for hours,' said Bean.

'No, we haven't,' I said.

'**Days,**' said Bean. He flicked another marshmallow into the air. '**CENTURIES.**'

'What's PADRRU like?' I asked Nix, who looked like she was trying to pretend that Bean didn't exist.

'Bet it's **BOR-ING**,' said Bean loudly.

I wondered if it was possible to invent something that would make Bean **STOP TALKING**.

'Not *bor-ing* at all, Earthling,' said Nix. '**PADRRU** is the most elite **INTER-GALACTIC PROTECTION FORCE** across all the galaxies. Thousands apply from each planet every year. Only a select few pass the examinations.'

'*Examinations?*' said Bean.

'**DOUBLE BOR-ING.**'

'We are tested in planetary cultures, planetary history, planetary languages and geography – if you want to join **PADRRU**, you must pass them all. To be selected is the highest honour.'

Bean sniggered. '*To be selected is the highest honour,*' he mimicked.

Oh for goodness' sake. How was I, Esha Verma, **genius inventor** extraordinaire, supposed to have an **INTELLIGENT** conversation with one of the COOLEST people I had ever met, when I was being interrupted by Broccoli's **DUNG-DROPPING** of a cousin every two seconds?

'Will you stop it, Bean?' I said.

'*Will you stop it, Bean?*' echoed Bean.

I glared at him. 'That's not funny, Bean.'

'That's not funny, Bean.'

I glanced towards my apprentice. Instead of doing something helpful about his IRRITANT of a cousin, he was standing at the back of the buggy, fiddling with the Two-way Talkie. Unfortunately, Bean had seen him too. Before I could stop him, he whipped out a marshmallow and PINGED it towards him. Archibald poked his head out, his eyes widening as the marshmallow looped across the air and <u>hit</u> Broccoli's hand.

The Two-way Talkie **bounced** out of Broccoli's grasp and disappeared into the mist.

Gone. For ever.

(Or so I thought.)

'No!' Broccoli shouted. 'That's our only link with Earth!'

Then, without a moment's hesitation, and to my complete amazement, he climbed onto the edge of the buggy and leapt into the mist after the Two-way Talkie.

The Lava Marsh
[written mostly by Broccoli]

I landed on the rocky ground, Esha's cries echoing behind me.

'BROCCOLI!' she shouted. 'NIX, STOP THE BUGGY! BROCCOLI'S GONE OVERBOARD!'

I stomped forward and squinted through the mist for the talkie, but it was impossible. The mist twisted and curled around my feet and legs, hiding the ground completely.

'NIX, DID YOU HEAR ME?' I could still hear Esha's voice somewhere behind me. 'YOU HAVE TO STOP THE BUGGY!'

'Can you see it, Archie?' I said.

No answer. He must have gone to sleep.

[A note from Esha: Or he was still sulking.]

'Esha, I need the Glo-Pr–' I called, turning back. But the buggy was no longer there. The mist had completely swallowed it up.

I licked my lips. Maybe
jumping off the buggy
hadn't been the best idea.
I could already imagine
what Bean would say about it - especially after I'd told him off
for not being careful. I sighed. I'd been so sure that becoming a
big brother would be exciting, but looking after Bean was no fun
at all.

Esha's voice floated through the mist again.

'BROCCOLI!'

'Esha! I'm here!'

'Where?'

'Here!'

'Could you be a little more SPECIFIC?'

I scanned the mist for landmarks. Then - POP!

I jumped as a column of fiery liquid burst
into the air some distance away from me.

Then . . .

POP! POP!

I gulped. Around me, the ground was coming
alive. Columns of blazing liquid burst into the air,
illuminating the mist in fountains of light.

I looked down at my feet. This was no ordinary mist.

I was standing on a LAVA MARSH.

POP! POP!

'ESHA!' I bellowed. 'Bean?'

'Broccoli!' Esha's voice thundered through the mist.

'Broccoli, we're on a lava marsh! RUN!'

'RUN WHERE?' I yelled. 'I CAN'T SEE YOU!'

'Here!'

Suddenly, through the spirals of mist, I spotted them. A cluster of golden lights blinking at me like fireflies. 'FOLLOW THE LIGHT!'

I hesitated, scanning the mist for the Two-way Talkie, but it was impossible to see anything.

POP!
POP!

The ground started to glow pink a few paces to the left of me. Then it shuddered, the vibrations so fierce that I could feel them through my toes.

Any moment now, the lava was going to blow.

Clutching Archibald, I sprinted towards the buggy (I am not sure why inventing always requires so much running). The ground cracked either side of me with a deafening POP! POP!

Around me, the columns of lava were growing closer. Each one burst into the sky with a delighted hissing noise, sparks spinning through the air like snakes.

Trying to ignore the noise, I pounded across the marsh, the circles of light bobbing unsteadily in the distance.

'HURRY UP, BROCCOLI!' shouted Esha.

'Use those legs, snot-face!' yelled Bean.

Archibald peered up at me, his eyes full of fear.

'It's OK, Archie,' I panted. 'We're going to make it.'

POP!

POP!

I glanced back over my shoulder and immediately wished I hadn't. The ground was ripping open, bright bursts of lava erupting through the marsh with heart-stopping speed.

I scrabbled through my pockets before remembering that the only invention I had with me was the Orange Marmalade Spray. Useful, but not exactly designed for a situation like this. Molten lava and marmalade seemed like a bad combination.

POP! POP!

Archibald ducked back into his shell, his whole body quaking.

POP! POP!

The air was growing hotter by the second. Sweat (or maybe snot) clung to my face as I powered towards the buggy. Esha was already hanging over the edge, her hand outstretched towards me.

'COME ON, BROCCOLI!'

POP! POP!

Another lava column burst into the air behind me.

'I'm not being sizzled for you, Broccoli!' yelled Bean. 'Hurry up!'

POP! POP!

With the last bit of energy I had left, I leapt into the air and grabbed hold of Esha's hand.

'Go!' shouted Bean over his shoulder.

With a loud VHRUM-THRUM-VHRUM, the buggy sprang forward, a fountain of lava exploding a hand's width behind us.

'HOLD ON TO YOUR STOCKINGS!' shouted Nix.

'PULL ME UP!' I shouted. My legs scrabbled against the side of the buggy, the air stinging my cheeks as we whizzed along.

'What - does - it - look - like - I'm - doing?' panted Esha, her face flushed with effort as she tried to hoist me onto the buggy. 'Bean, help me.'

Bean folded his arms across his chest. 'Why should I?'

'BEAN!' shouted Esha.

The buggy jolted and spun through the mist, spouts of lava erupting in all directions.

Bean rolled his eyes. 'Fine. But I'm not saving you for nothing, bore-brain. You owe me after this, understand? You. Owe. Me.'

I could feel my hand slipping from Esha's grasp. 'JUST PULL ME UP!'

'OK, OK,' muttered Bean, grabbing hold of my sleeve.

'On three,' shouted Esha. 'THREE!'

With a fierce tug, they yanked me over the side of the buggy. I collapsed onto the deck, gulping great lungfuls of air as I tried to catch my breath.

'Good to have you back, Broccoli,' said Esha, thumping me on the arm.

'Heeuthghghghtth,' I murmured (I was trembling too much to speak).

'My thoughts exactly,' she said.

'Shouldn't have jumped off the buggy,' said Bean, smirking down at me.

'I - didn't - do - it - for - fun,' I gasped. 'I was trying to get the talkie.'

'So much for looking after me,' said Bean. He twirled his slingshot into the air and strutted off. 'You can't even look after yourself.'

I staggered to my feet. Bursts of molten lava spewed into the air around us as we raced forward, Nix manoeuvring the buggy frantically between them.

'How much further to the ship?' shouted Esha.

'Do not speak to me, Earthling!' yelled Nix. 'I am BUSY!'

That's when the buggy made a CHUG-CHUG noise.

It was not a happy CHUG-CHUG noise.

It was the sort of CHUG-CHUG noise that made my nose quiver.

'Er - Nix?' I said. 'What is that?'

CHUG-CHUG-CHUG.

CHUG-CHUG-CHUG.

Nix was staring at the console, eyes wide. 'No, nada, no, these engine readings cannot be right. We should still have full power—'

CHUG-CHUG-CHUG.

CHUG-CHUG-CHUG.

The buggy jerked forward a couple of times, then came to a sudden, heart-stopping halt.

Meanwhile, Back on Earth . . .

(told mostly by Nishi)

I shook the talkie. 'Hello? Broccoli? Esha?'

Beside my desk, Berty whined.

'Don't look at me like that,' I said, glaring at

him. 'You're the one who knocked a glass of

water over this thing.' I swivelled the dial a few

times. 'Hello? Anyone there?'

Silence.

I thought for a moment about what Esha had said. An alien

had come onto Earth and taken her identity? No way. Esha and

Broccoli were winding me up. They had to be. They were probably in

Esha's room right now, giggling away.

And I'd had enough.

Throwing down my pen, I opened my door, stormed

across the landing, and barged straight into Esha's room.

She was sitting at her desk, bent over a notebook.

'Oh, so you are here, are you?' I snapped. 'I thought you were

on a different planet.'

152

Esha looked up, a thick smear of blueberry juice around her mouth. She gave me a sickeningly sweet smile. 'Hello, dear sister,' she said.

'Do you think you're funny, Esha?' I retorted. 'Because I'm NOT laughing. Telling me a load of lies about aliens is not funny.' I looked around the room. 'Where's Broccoli?'

'Brocc-o-li?'

'Let me guess. He's already left, has he? Well, you tell him that if he tries anything like that again, I'm telling his parents. Some of us have important work to do — like writing weather reports — so stop bothering me!'

There was a low growl behind me. I turned around to find Berty glaring at Esha, his eyes NARROWED into thin slits.

 'Berty?' I said.

He growled again, louder this time.

I glanced at Esha, who was scowling at Berty. I had never seen her look at him like that before.

'It is fortunate that you are here, dear sister,' said Esha. 'I wanted to speak with you. This super-market. It did not keep Zirboonium.'

'Zirboonium?' I said. 'What are you talking about? Why would there be Zirboonium at the supermarket?'

'There is Zirboonium on this planet, is there not?' Esha said, a touch of worry in her voice.

I snorted. 'Is that a joke? You've only told me about it a gazillion times.' I put on a shrill Esha voice. 'England is the only country in the whole world with Zirboonium ... blah blah; Zirboonium is so cool, blah-boring-blah; it's going to be in town on the tenth of July ...'

'It is?' said Esha, her face brightening. 'Where is it being kept if not in the super-market?'

'You should know — you're always going on about it. Zirboonium this — Zirboonium that. Zirboonium I–DON'T–CARE, so stop disturbing me.'

I turned around and stormed back to my room, Berty following close behind me.

'She thinks she's so funny,' I grumbled. 'Well she's not.' I slammed the door shut.

Berty growled at the door and thumped his tail against the carpet.

[A note from Esha: This was Berty trying to communicate. Unfortunately, my sister is too much of a DRONG to notice.]

I stared at Berty and chewed my lip. As much as I wanted to ignore Esha and Broccoli's story about an alien, I couldn't shake the feeling that there was something ODD going on. In fact, there were a few odd things going on. Esha's strangely polite behaviour, the blueberries, all the questions about Zirboonium — and then there was Berty, who was still growling at the door. He never growled at Esha. EVER. In fact, I'd never known him to growl at anyone. Not even the postman.

'You don't think . . . ?' I began, looking down at him. Then I shook my head. NO. Esha was just being as annoying as always. No way had she been replaced by an alien from a planet called

Zelpha. That was ridiculous, even for her. This was part of some elaborate plan that she'd concocted with Broccoli to wind me up. As if they hadn't ruined my life enough already.

Well, I wasn't going to fall for it — no matter how WEIRDLY she behaved.

Ultra-Umbrellas, or How Not to Fly a Planet Buggy

'GONE!' shrieked Nix. 'The engine is kaput!'
Sweltering spouts of lava exploded all
around us, each one sounding LOUDER
and angrier than the one before.

pOp! pOp!

'How is this possible?' She jabbed the console
desperately. 'We had enough power to reach the ship!'

pOp! pOp!

The engine sputtered, the buggy
limping forward like a sick fish before
stopping again.

I glared at Broccoli, who sniffed guiltily and
looked down at his shoes.

Nix punched the console with her fist. The
engine made a LOUD choking noise, then fell
silent.

'It's not working,' said Bean unhelpfully.

'We will have to abandon the buggy,' declared Nix, turning towards us. 'Prepare to run, Earthlings!

Run or be SIZZLED!'

'Run?' said Broccoli incredulously. Fountains of pink and purple lava ricocheted into the air, growing closer and closer by the second. 'We can't run through that. We'll **NEVER** make it!'

pOp!

pOp!

'Broccoli's right,' I said. 'If we abandon the buggy, we'll never make it through and we'll never stop Goospa before The Optimum Time. We need a Plan B.' I gave Nix my most positive smile. 'Fortunately, I, Esha Verma, am a known EXPERT at Plan Bs. Isn't that right, Broccoli?'

'Uh—'

pOp! pOp! pOp!

I pulled out two cylindrical objects and waved them proudly at Nix. 'The Ultra-Umbrella. Designed for all weathers. Foldable, portable, height-adjustable—'

(In case you, the Reader, are wondering, I, Esha Verma, **genius inventor**, only built a weather-inspired invention

because of a bet with my DRONG of a sister. She claimed an all-weather umbrella could **never** exist – and she was **MISTAKEN**.)

'How is an *umbrella* going to help us?' said Bean.

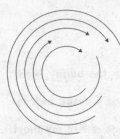

'—with rapid **ROTARY** motion. We don't need to abandon the buggy. We can take it **UP!**'

'Um-brel-la?' Nix blinked at me. She had an even better unimpressed face than Nishi. 'What is an um-brel-la?'

'It's—' began Bean.

'What's going to get us out of here,' I interrupted quickly (somehow, I had a feeling that Nix would be less keen on my idea if she knew what umbrellas were (actually) for).

pOp! pOp! pOp!

More lava columns erupted into the air around us. Nix glanced over her shoulder, her face paling as the ground shook apart.

'This plan of yours **better work,** Earthling. Otherwise we are all quozzled.'

'It'll work,' I said, pulling out a bundle of string and tape. 'I'm not a **genius inventor** for nothing, you know.' I passed an Ultra-Umbrella to Broccoli. 'Secure it to the back rail. I'll take the front.'

'But . . . don't you remember what happened last time?' whispered Broccoli. 'The motor jammed.'

pOp! pOp!

'That was the second prototype, Broccoli,' I *hissed*. 'This is the third. There's not a teensy-tiny chance of it jamming. Now hurry up!'

pOp! pOp! pOp!

Broccoli sniffed and darted towards the other side of the buggy.

Meanwhile, I pushed the **RELEASE** button on my umbrella. A handle shot out of the tail end. I secured it around the rail; then I pressed a second button above it. A moment later, the rest of the umbrella **shot into the air** in a

RELEASE

spellbinding spectacle of salmon pink.

'Ready, Broccoli?' I called.

He sniffed, which I took to mean yes.

'Fire it up!'

I slammed the **MAXIMUM HEIGHT** button. The umbrella **shot** even further into the air until it was high above my head.

Nix blinked. 'What in the planetary—'

'That's it!' I yelled, as Broccoli's umbrella did the same. 'Bring on the *rapid rotary motion!*' I pressed the **GO** button.

With a **LOUD** *whirr*, the Ultra-Umbrellas began to spin. The buggy rattled sideways, **trembling** with the force of our beauteous brollies.

'Come on, come on,' I muttered.

But the buggy remained on the ground. The lava columns were growing **closer.**

pOp! pOp!

'It is not working, Earthling!' cried Nix. 'We should have abandoned the buggy like I said!'

'Increase the power, Broccoli!' I shouted, turning up the dial. 'All the way to **Extreme Weather!'**

The umbrella propellers *whirred* faster, the buggy quivering around us.

Then, with a

glorious **WHOOSH,** we rose into the air and . . .

$\Rightarrow$ (stopped.) $\Leftarrow$

We were hovering just above the ground, the umbrellas straining with the effort.

'What's happening?' shouted Bean.

'THE BUGGY'S TOO HEAVY!'

I bellowed. 'We have to REDUCE the **WEIGHT!**'

 Archibald jerked his head towards Bean as if to say, 'You know (who) to sacrifice.'

'The lights,' murmured Nix. 'Dump the lights! You – silly Earthling!' She motioned at Bean. 'You take that side.'

'What did you just call me?' said Bean.

'MOVE!'

Nix dashed between the lights on the left of the buggy, whipping open their knots and shoving them over the side. 'Faster, Earthling,' she ordered, flitting past Bean, who was still struggling with the first lantern. 'Quick like the silver!'

pOp! pOp! pOp!

We were starting to rise again.

'It's working!' I shouted. With a glorious uplift, the buggy rose higher and higher, the whole contraption

RATTLING

and CREAKING

as the Ultra-Umbrellas took us into the air. 'We're flying!' hollered Bean. He scooted to the edge of the buggy and _whooped_ in delight.

'We're REALLY FLYING!!'

(In my genius opinion, Bean was only *half* correct. The buggy wasn't just flying. It was *soaring*!)

'Air currents,' said Nix. 'The higher we go, the faster they will become. Quick like the silver. Unless anything goes wrong.'

'We've trialled and tested these Ultra-Umbrellas over ten times,' I said, giving Nix a reassuring smile. 'Not a chance that they would—'

That's when the umbrella above me gave a short, sharp sputter. It whirred awkwardly, the motor clicking like a wheezy grasshopper.

UH OH.

My stomach did a little flip.

'It's jammed!' I exclaimed.

The buggy dipped suddenly sideways, the other umbrella struggling against the weight.

'It's not going to hold!' yelled Broccoli. 'We need both of them! Unjam it!'

'I'm – trying!' I gasped, jabbing the GO button, but the umbrella stayed where it was. 'The whole thing's stuck!' I began frantically rummaging through my Inventor's Kit. 'I've got a spanner in here some—'

pOp!

A vicious flare of pink lava exp**loded** into the air and hit the front end of the buggy.

For one **toe-tingling** moment, nothing happened. The buggy stayed exactly where it was, almost as if it was too shocked to move.

Then . . .

we . . .

began to **SPIN** . . .

and **TWIST** . . .

the buggy spiralling

UNCONTROLLABLY

through the air currents.

'The umbrellas can't hold us!' I yelled, clutching onto the umbrella rod. The buggy spun around me in a blur of colour. 'We're too **unstable!**'

'**WAHOOOO!**' whooped Bean. '**THIS IS BRILL—**' He slipped and fell, shooting straight off the deck and disappearing out of sight. A second later, he reappeared, his face flushed with effort as he clung to the buggy.

'HEEEELLLPPP!' shouted Bean.
'HEEELLP ME!'

'BEAN, HANG ON!' bellowed Broccoli. 'I'LL BE RIGHT THERE!'

'BROCCOLI, WHAT ARE YOU **DOING?**' I yelled as my *sniffly* apprentice **wobbled** towards his cousin. 'STAY WHERE YOU ARE!'

The buggy SWIVELLED...

and...

swirled...

so *violently* that Broccoli also lost his balance and hurtled across the deck. Archibald slipped out of his hands and landed on the buggy's rail...

'ARCHIE!' thundered Broccoli, clinging on to the side of the buggy. 'WAIT THERE!' His tortoise swayed on the spot, teetering dangerously close to the edge. 'I'M COMING!'

'HEEEELLPP!' shrieked Bean. 'I - can't - hold - on - much - longer!'

Broccoli looked frantically from his tortoise to Bean then back again, his snot swinging. And, OK, I am sure that you, the Reader, are thinking this was the best time to come up with a GENIUS IDEA, but we were moving so fast that I could hardly even hear myself THINK. Instead, I did something that was probably not very genius at all.

'GET BEAN!' I shouted. 'I'LL TAKE CARE OF ARCHIBALD!'

Taking a deep breath, I let go of the umbrella rod and threw myself towards Archibald.

At least, I tried. The buggy danced wildly, sending me flying in the other direction. I slid sideways as we spun out of the mist and the marsh, across the pink sky.

Silver streaks of light *whizzed* past my head

as we swirled

AROUND
and
AROUND

the buggy twisting
against the currents...

'HEEEELLLPP!' yelled Bean.

'I should **NEVER** have listened to you Earthlings!'
bellowed Nix. 'You are as foolish as—'

But I never heard what she said next – because at that
moment I was thrown OFF the buggy.

A Discovery

Down I fell...

the currents whipping my breath away...

d

o

w

d

n...

o

w

n... my genius life

 whizzing before my eyes...

(again)

... and I was *absolutely* certain that this was the moment
that I, Esha Verma, **genius inventor** extraordinaire,
was about to become a genius **SPLAT** ...

when ...

(take a breath, Reader)

... I landed with an

ENORMOUS
PLOP

into a river of COLD, **purple** sludge ...

'YAAAAGH!' I burst out of the **sludge**, coughing and spluttering as I swam to the edge and collapsed onto the rock. It was a couple of moments before I could sit up.

'Hello?' I said, my voice sounding oddly quiet. I cleared my throat and tried again, louder this time. 'HELLO?'

Nothing.

All I could hear was the low **GLUG-GLUG** of the river in front of me.

'Broccoli? Nix? Bean?'

There was no sign of them – or the buggy – anywhere.

All I could see was:

① A river of wet purple **sludge**.

② Purple rock.

③ A string of crooked grey stumps along the riverbank.

④ Exactly **ZERO** clues about where the others might be.

I shivered.

Could the buggy have

FALLEN in the RIVER?

No. I pushed all thoughts of splatting and **CRASHING** out of my mind. Instead, I took off my shoes, shook out the sludge and slid them back on, wincing at the unpleasant gloopy sensation between my toes. Then I stood up and cupped my hands around my mouth.

'HELLO?' I shouted again. 'BROCCOLI? BEAN? NIX?'

The river glug-glugged back at me.

I looked up at the sky again, hoping that the buggy might suddenly *appear*, but it remained empty.

'They'll be fine,' I said aloud, ignoring the sinking sensation in my stomach. Being on a different planet was **NOT** fun when you were alone. Not even for a **genius**

inventor. '*Completely* fine. I'm sure I can figure out where they are.' I took out a bar of chocolate from my pocket and nibbled on the top (the *Inventor's Handbook* says that *chocolate can be a useful way of generating ideas*).

[A note from Broccoli: I don't remember that part.]

Unfortunately, at that moment the chocolate didn't appear to be working. Maybe it was because it tasted of sludge. I

ate it anyway. Then I pulled out a couple
of cookies and *ate* those too.

By the time I was done, I was feeling a teensy-tiny
bit sick and I still had exactly ZERO clues about how to
locate the buggy.

Just then, in the not-so-far distance, I heard a shout.

A Broccoli-like shout.

'Broccoli!' I sprinted through the grey stumps
towards the sound, my shoes making a horrible noise as I
ran. **SQUELCH-SQUELCH**. 'Hang on – I'm coming!'
I panted as I sped out of the stumps.

There, in the centre of a rocky clearing, with his back
to me, was my **sniffly, sludge-covered** apprentice.
A **bubble** of relief rose inside me . . . and p⁰pped almost
instantaneously as I caught sight of the creature
in **front** of him.

A familiar, tall creature

with long spindly arms and legs.

'GOOSPA?' I exclaimed.

Broccoli backed away from Goospa to stand beside me.

'Broccoli, what happened?' I whispered. 'Where's Bean and Nix and Archibald?'

'Nix and I were **thrown** off the buggy. The other two stayed on. I climbed out of the river and found *him*.'

I stared at Goospa, my brain **bursting** with questions. 'How did you get here?' I sputtered. Then, 'Actually, I don't care about that. I want to have words with you! Very important words! I don't know what rules they have on Zelpha, but on Earth you can't go around **shapeshifting** into people and you especially can't shapeshift into ME!

I'm a **genius inventor** and I'm Do you understand?'

Goospa blinked at me for a moment. He looked down at himself, covered in purple river **sludge**. Then he rolled his eyes.

I took a step closer to Goospa. 'Do you know where the others are?' I said.

Goospa's only answer was to **shake** himself, sending bits of purple sludge flying in all directions.

'Hey!' I shouted, ducking as a blob whizzed past my cheek. 'I asked you a question!'

'Esha,' murmured Broccoli. He was staring at Goospa with a peculiar expression on his face. His snot dropped a centimetre. 'I don't think that's Goospa. Look at the robes. Goospa's were orange, not yellow.'

I shook my head in disbelief. 'Course it's him. Who else would it be?'

'No, nada, no,' the creature said in a voice that sounded oddly familiar. 'It is not.'

I blinked. A horrible _ICY SHIVER_ ran down my back. 'What did you just—'

But now the creature was transforming. Exactly as Goospa had in the shed, only quicker – their head shot down, their arms and legs slid inwards. Their whole body trembled and twisted with such force that small puffs of purple dust shot into the air. A bright light shone around them, forcing me to shield my eyes and step back.

'Esha, look,' breathed Broccoli. 'I told you it wasn't Goospa.'

I blinked at the person now standing in front of us.

She was wearing colourful trousers, sparkly boots and a red blazer with pockets on the sleeves.

The coolest blazer I had ever seen.

'Nix?' I said hesitantly. 'Is that you?'

'What does it look like, Earthling?' she snapped.

'But I don't understand! You looked exactly like Goospa!' I exclaimed.

'I am nothing like that fungus-weed.' Nix bristled. 'It is true what we learn about you Earthlings. You do not care for detail. Goospa and I look entirely different.' She tweaked the sleeves of her blazer. 'Goospa is a – a . . . What do you Earthlings call it? A dung-beetle.' Her nose wrinkled. 'My dung-beetle of a younger brother.'

'Brother?' said Broccoli in disbelief. 'You're one of Goospa's four hundred and ninety-nine brothers and sisters?'

'Correct, Earthling.' Nix stood up a little taller. 'To be precise, I am the Crown Princess of the Planet Zelpha, of the Triweeni Cluster in the NEWPORLA DIMENSION. Exact co-ordinates: 3xyz-890-12wez.'

I g°ggled. 'You're the Crown Princess of Zelpha?'

'Indeed.'

'You can *shapeshift*,' I said. 'Just like him.'

'No. My shapeshifting skills are **far superior**,' said Nix. 'He is **slow** – **clumsy** – **bread-fingered** – a – a –' she waved her hand in the air as if she was searching for words –

'a galumphing stumblebum.

An embarrassment.'

'He did a good job of shapeshifting into Esha,' said Broccoli.

My brain had so many questions that I was quite certain it was going to COMBUST. 'I don't understand. You're Goospa's sister?'

'Correct,' said Nix. She flicked a blob of sludge off her arm. 'You Earthlings really are one of the least intelligent species in all the galaxies. It is a wonder you still have a planet.'

'But you said you work for PADRRU,' I said.

'The Planetary and Dimensional Rapid Response Unit. You track down criminals. Don't you?'

Nix hesitated.

'So you don't work for PADRRU?' I said, unable to hide the disappointment from my voice. I'd thought that Nix was the coolest person I had ever met. I'd thought she had the coolest job I'd ever heard of (second only to being a genius inventor). Now it turned out that she was a liar. A shapeshifting sneak.

'Does PADRRU even exist?' said Broccoli.

Nix scowled. 'Of course it exists, Earthling. Being a member of the Planetary and Dimensional Rapid Response Unit is the highest honour. Far better than being a crown princess.' She spat out the words as if they left a sour taste in her mouth. 'I passed the most difficult examinations in the entire galaxy and was offered a job – a true honour.

But The Ma and The Pa refused to let me take it.
An unsuitable profession for the Crown Princess of

Zelpha, they said. All they care about is royal duties.'

'So how did you end up chasing Goospa if you don't even work for **PADRRU**?' asked Broccoli.

'If you must know, I was running away from my planet to join **PADRRU** when Goospa interfered with my plans,' said Nix coldly. 'He said he wanted my ship. I was ejected before I could stop him.'

'Bean was right,' I said. 'He said that we shouldn't trust you. ➡ **You're a LIAR!**' ⬅

'It was not all lies,' said Nix sharply. 'It is true that if Goospa attempts to teleport your planet, the entire galaxy is in *danger*. I will apprehend him and escort him to **PADRRU**.'

I folded my arms across my chest and glared at her. 'Why should we believe a single word you say when you've been pretending to be someone else?' Saying the words out loud made me realize how **angry** I was.

Angry at Goospa for stranding us on a No-Go planet, angry at Nix for lying to us, but mostly angry at myself for believing her in the first place.

'What was I supposed to do?' said Nix. 'I know all about you Earthlings. If I had not taken this form, if I had told you who I really was, you would never have trusted me.'

'You don't know that,' said Broccoli quietly.

'He's right,' I said. 'You didn't even give us a chance. You say you know about Earthlings. Have you even visited Earth?'

Nix flushed.

'You haven't, have you?' I said. 'You think you know all about Earthlings, but you're wrong. You should have told us the truth from the start instead of lying to us. How come you shapeshifted back anyway?'

'Because I fell into this repulsive river,' said Nix. 'Liquid temporarily reverses our current form. Earthlings, we have no time to lose. We need to work together to get off this planet and find Goospa. You cannot do that alone.'

'Watch us,' I said. Even the thought of working with that lying sneak Nix a moment longer made me want to PUKE.

Broccoli grabbed hold of my arm and pulled me to one side. 'She's right, Esha,' he whispered. 'We need her *help*.'

'She **lied** to us,' I said in a low voice. 'Maybe she and Goospa are in it together. She could be distracting us here while he builds his teleportation device!'

Broccoli *sniffed* and shook his head. 'I don't think so. Call it inventor's instinct, but I think she's telling us the truth now.'

I glanced at Nix. She was watching us with a **worried expression** on her face. I sighed. Deep down, I knew that my *sniffly* apprentice was right. Nix might have lied to us about who she was, but I believed she was telling the truth about everything else.

'We need to stop Goospa, and the only way we can do that is by getting back to Earth on her ship,' said Broccoli. He checked his watch. 'It's 1.30 p.m. now. That means we've only got **TWO HOURS LEFT** until The Optimum Time.'

'Doesn't look like we've got **much choice**,' I said crossly.

[A note from Broccoli: This is what my dad calls a stalemate.]

Nix was no longer watching us. Instead, she had taken

out a square device from her pocket and was staring at it closely. She looked up as we approached her.

'**Well?**' she said in an **ULTRA**-irritating voice. 'Have you Earthlings decided how you will be leaving this planet all by yourselves? I cannot *wait* to hear your plan.

Your umbrellas worked *so* well.'

 I glared at her in silence, every bit of me fizzing with annoyance. I didn't trust myself to say anything.

'We'll come with you,' said Broccoli.

'As I thought,' said Nix haughtily. She tapped the device in her hand. 'I have located the buggy. The good news is that it is not far.'

'What about Bean and Archibald?' said Broccoli.

'What about them?'

'Have you located them too?'

'I have no way of knowing if the silly Earthling and the shell-creature are still **inside** the buggy.'

Broccoli paled, his snot dropping anxiously. 'You don't?'

'No,' said Nix. 'With any luck, they are not. The silly Earthling was most infuriating.'

185

My heart sank. But I wasn't going to let Nix know that. I'd just about had enough of her.

'They are not a silly Earthling and a shell-creature,' I said firmly. 'Their names are Bean and Archibald, and they'll be on the buggy.

I'm 110% certain of it.'

A Different Kind
of Lightbulb Moment

Nix, Broccoli and I trudged through the grey stumps across

the purple rock. To our right, the sludge

river glug-glugged loudly. To our left,

beyond the stumps,

the planet stretched out endlessly,

the ground bumpier
than a pine cone.

Above us, the sky gleamed pink, flashes of green
and silver light illuminating the stumps around us with a
strange glow.

Nix marched ahead, the tracker held out in front of her.

'I should have done a better job of looking after Bean
and Archibald,' said Broccoli miserably. 'Aunt Wendy and
Granny Bertha would be so disappointed in me. What if . . .'
He hesitated, his bottom lip trembling as if he was about
to cry.

'They'll be OK, Broccoli,' I interrupted firmly.
'Bean might be the **MOST** annoying pustule ever, but he's smart.'

'You really think so?' said Broccoli.

I nodded.

(OK, I wasn't 100% convinced about Bean's intelligence, but I thought it best not to tell Broccoli that.)

'So is Archibald,' I went on. 'He's survived a Guzzler and a **weathernova,** remember? He's one of the sneakiest—cleverest reptiles I know.'

Broccoli looked slightly brighter. 'You're right. They'll be fine. Totally fine,' he repeated, almost as if he was trying to convince himself. He shivered and rubbed his arms. 'It's getting colder.'

'Temperature will continue to drop' said Nix without turning around. 'If we do not reach my ship before it gets **dark,** we shall *freeze* to ice creams.'

Broccoli sneezed. 'That doesn't sound good. How long till it gets dark?'

(I kept quiet. I wanted to know that too, but I had decided that I would only talk to Nix as a matter of **COMPLETE AND ABSOLUTE NECESSITY.**)

'Not long,' said Nix, pointing. Above us, the sky glimmered silver, green, then silver again. 'These shifts in colour and the drop in temperature indicate that night will be falling soon. We must hurry.'

We continued walking, the air growing colder and colder until, suddenly, Nix gave a shout and sprinted ahead. There, not far in the distance, was the buggy.

Or, at least, what was left of it.

The front half was sunken in the sludgy river. The rest of it was wedged on the surrounding rock. The half that we could see did not look good.

NOT ONE BIT.

The wheels had fallen off, the rail had broken, and the wood had splintered. The entire contraption creaked and groaned against the force of the river.

'Rapids of The Rumba Stars,' growled Nix.

She laid a hand on the side of the buggy, then glared at us.
'Look what you Earthlings did to my buggy! This was gifted
to me on my . . .'

But I wasn't listening to her. Like Broccoli, I was too
busy *staring* at the wreck. A horrible cold feeling had
settled in the pit of my stomach. Surely no one could
have survived such a **terrible crash?**

'BEAN?'

yelled Broccoli.

'ARCHIBALD?'

I had never heard him **SHOUT** so loudly before.
'BEAN, WHERE ARE YOU? ARCHIBALD, CAN YOU *HEAR ME?*'
He raced around the buggy, disappearing out of view.

'Are you listening to me, Earthling?' said Nix. 'My buggy
has been **ruined** because of you.'

'I don't care,' I retorted. 'We've got bigger things to
worry about right now. Like finding Bean and Archibald!'

'Find them?' Nix shook her head. 'Look at this buggy.
Do you really think we will find them? No, **nada, no.**'

Without another word, I pushed past her and sprinted round the buggy. My apprentice was sitting against the edge of the wreck with his head in his hands.

'Broccoli?' I said.

Nothing.

I stepped forward and touched his arm.

He looked up. His eyes were wet and there was a trail of snot snaking down his cheek.

'They're not here,' he said quietly.

I hesitated. The *Inventor's Handbook* had prepared me for many situations, but this was (not) one of them. In fact, at that moment, I didn't have a teensy-tiny idea what to say or do. I tried desperately to think of something, anything.

'Well,' I said. 'Maybe we should look—'

'WAHOOOOOOOO!'

My head shot towards the sound. So did Broccoli's.

'WAHOOOOOOOO!'

'Is that . . . Bean?' I said.

With a supreme sniff, Broccoli leapt to his feet and ran towards the noise. **'BEAN?'** he thundered. **'BEAN, IS THAT** *YOU?'*

'Wait – I'm coming, too!' I shouted, speeding after him as he raced away from the river into the cluster of grey stumps ahead of us.

'Where do you think you are going?' called Nix after us. 'Come back here at once! I am speaking to you, Earthlings, and I demand that you—'

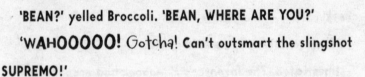

'BEAN?' yelled Broccoli. 'BEAN, WHERE ARE YOU?'

'WAHOOOOO! Gotcha! Can't outsmart the slingshot SUPREMO!'

'This way, Broccoli!' I shouted, diving to my left.

Panting, we came to a halt in a small clearing. A short distance ahead of us, his slingshot aimed at a grey stump, was a ~~sludge monster~~ sludge-covered Bean. BLOP!

A marshmallow whizzed through the air and hit the stump. Something orange fell to the ground. 'WAHOOO!'

I grinned. I had never been so glad to see Broccoli's annoying zit of a cousin in my entire life.

'BEAN!' Broccoli sprinted forward and pulled him into a

hug. 'You're OK!'

There was a sequence of muffled groans, then Bean pulled himself away, his face twisted in disgust. 'Of course I'm OK! How many times do I have to tell you? I don't need you to look after me!'

'Do you have any idea how *worried* I was?' said Broccoli. 'I thought something had happened to you!'

'Well, you were wrong,' said Bean. He bent down, scooped the orange thing off the ground and stuffed it into his mouth. 'As usual,' he continued, spitting orange bits at us.

'What are you eating?' I said.

'Don't know,' said Bean, chomping loudly. 'They grow on these stumps. Took me a while to spot them because they're so high up. They look like berries, but they taste like cheese.'

'You shouldn't be eating those,' said Broccoli. 'You don't know if they're safe.'

Bean threw a couple more into his mouth. '*Not bad* actually,' he said, ignoring him completely.

Broccoli sighed. 'Where's Archibald?'

'Archibald?' Bean **stared** at him. 'How would I know? Isn't he with you?'

'No,' said Broccoli. 'He was on the buggy with you.' His snot **wobbled**. 'You – you mean he's *not here?*'

Bean looked at him with the **MOST SERIOUS** of **SERIOUS FACES** and shook his head.

'But this is . . . How can . . .' began Broccoli.

Suddenly Bean **giggled**. 'Got you, **bore-brain!** Your tortoise is over there.' He waved towards a green **blob** on a rock behind him. 'That means you owe me **twice**. *Once* for saving you, and *once* for saving your silly pet.'

'That wasn't funny, Bean!' said Broccoli. He darted towards Archibald and lifted him up, examining him carefully. 'You OK, Archie?' he said.

'You found them!' said Nix, puffing to a stop behind us.

'Told you we would,' I said. 'Thanks for all the help, by the way.' I gave her an **ULTRA-RUDE** look. 'Us feeble-brained Earthlings couldn't have done it without you.'

Nix glowered at me. 'We do not have time for this **dally-dillying**. We have to find my ship before night falls.'

'How are we going to do that?' said Bean. 'Your buggy's *broken.*'

'I know that, Earthling,' said Nix coldly. 'We will *walk.* We will use this to locate the ship.' She held up the same square device that she had used to locate the buggy.

'BOR-ING. How long do we have to *walk?*' asked Bean.

'For as long as it takes,' said Nix. She turned to Broccoli, who was still peering at Archibald. 'Are you even listening, Earthling?'

'Archie?' said Broccoli. 'Wake up.' He looked at us. 'He's not moving,' he said anxiously.

It was true. Archibald was completely still, his eyes shut tight. ⌣⌣ There was a thin orange smudge around his mouth.

Broccoli glanced down at the rock; a few of the orange things that Bean had been eating were scattered across it.

Broccoli picked them up. 'Did you give him these to eat?'

Bean nodded. 'I thought he might be hungry too.'

The tips of Broccoli's ears had turned scarlet. 'We're on another planet! These could be **poisonous** for tortoises!'

195

'I'm eating them,' said Bean. More orange flecks whizzed out of his mouth into the air. 'Nothing wrong with me.'

He poked Archibald, who didn't move. 'He's probably just tired. He's a tortoise, remember? All they do is sleep.'

'Tortoises can't eat everything that HUMANS can eat!' exploded Broccoli. 'Don't you know ANYTHING?'

I was looking closely at Archibald. As I watched, he popped one crafty eye open. He glanced between Broccoli and Bean, a mischievous grin on his face, then he shut it again.

[A note from Broccoli: I am still quite certain that Esha was imagining things. Archibald would never pretend to be ill.]

'Er – Broccoli?' I said. 'I think that—'

But Broccoli wasn't listening.

'I can't believe I was worried about finding you,' he said, glaring at Bean. 'You've been a headache since we got here and now you've made Archie sick! I wish you'd never come. If it hadn't been for you tagging along, we'd have been at the ship by now. In fact, we probably wouldn't even have ended up on this planet in the first place.' His snot swung faster and faster as he spoke.

'Broccoli—' I said.

'It's **your** fault that we got thrown through that portal. I wish Aunt Wendy had never brought you. In fact, I wish **YOU** weren't my cousin.'

Bean stepped back in surprise, a look of *hurt* flickering across his face.

I tried again. 'I think Archibald is actually—'

'Well that makes two of us,' said Bean quietly.

'You're the **WORST** cousin **EVER,** *bore-brain,*

AND you'll be the **WORST BROTHER,** too.'

'At least I won't be YOURS,'

retorted Broccoli.

The words cracked through the air around us before hardening into a frosty silence.

Suddenly Nix's tracker made a shrill beeping noise.

'The ship is located,' she said. She looked between Bean and Broccoli, who were both glaring at each other, and scoffed. 'Family. Same in all galaxies.' She marched off towards the grey stumps to the right of us. 'This way, Earthlings.'

Bean shoved another handful of orange berries into his mouth, scowled at Broccoli, then **STOMPED** off after her.

I looked at Broccoli.

'What?' he said, stalking after them.

'Don't you think that was a bit – I don't know – **mean?'** I said, hurrying to keep up.

'Mean?' Broccoli goggled at me incredulously. 'Look at Archie! He's *unconscious!*' He held his EVIL tortoise close to his face. 'I've never seen him so pale!'

Archibald was still **not moving.**

☆ (Talk about an OSCAR-WINNING performance.) ☆☆

'He looks the same to me. Are you sure he's not—'

'What?' said Broccoli sharply.

'Well, maybe, he *is* just sleeping,' I said. Somehow, I didn't think telling Broccoli that Archibald was pretending was probably a **good idea**, at least not right now. 'And Bean was only trying to help.'

'Sure he was. Just like he was *trying to help* when he stole the Boomer from my room. Just like when he made me drop the Two-way Talkie into the lava marsh. Just like he's been *trying to help* the whole time we've been on this stupid planet!'

Broccoli was moving so fast that I was practically jogging to keep up with him. 'You were right, Esha,' he said. 'I should never have brought him to Inventor's HQ. It was a mistake. I don't know why Aunt Wendy thought I'd be good for him. Bean doesn't care about anyone but **himself**.'

'He did save Archie,' I pointed out, not entirely sure why I was bothering to defend Bean. 'He could have left him behind, but he didn't.'

Broccoli sniffed miserably, walking even faster. 'I can't

believe I was excited about having a baby brother.'
He shook his head. 'If he's anything like Bean,
I'd rather not have one.'

'That's not true,' I panted. 'Families might
be annoying, but there are **worse** things.'

Broccoli glanced at me in surprise. 'You're
the one who always says Nishi's a DRONG.
And that your parents don't understand your
genius.'

I opened my mouth to argue, then shut it again.
Broccoli was right.

[A note from Broccoli: I usually am.]

I was <u>always</u> complaining about Mum, Dad and Nishi.
Thinking about it, I suddenly realized that I wasn't that
different to Nix. OK, I wasn't a
PAMPERED princess and I hadn't run
away from home, but I didn't care about
my family like I should.

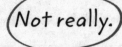

(Not really.)

Yes, Nishi might have been a DRONG to me on **COUNTLESS** occasions, but I shouldn't have stolen her tickets to the Central Research Laboratory (and I

 definitely should have said sorry afterwards). And I was **always** complaining about Mum and Dad not

understanding my genius, but I had never apologized for all the things I'd exploded or broken around the house (including

 IMPORTANT and EXPENSIVE stuff). I'd been too busy with my own inventions to worry about their feelings.

Now I was stuck on a No-Go planet and I might never get to see any of them again.

I swallowed.

I had experienced genius lightbulb moments many times, but this one was different. It was **horrible** and cold and left me with a feeling that was nothing like the spingly-tingly sort. Instead, it felt a lot like the

I've-messed-up-really-badly kind.

I just hoped it wasn't (too late) to put things right.

How I, Nishi Verma,
Made an <u>Important</u> Discovery

(told mostly by Nishi Verma)

KNOCK! KNOCK!

`Busy,' I said, without looking up from

my weather report.

Thursday
+20°

There was another knock.

Berty peeped out from under my legs and growled at the door.

`I said, I'm BUSY!'

A pause, then – KNOCK! KNOCK!

FOR GOODNESS' SAKE.

I yanked my door open.

`Hello, dear sister,' said Esha.

She smiled at me. The kind of smile that

a shark might give before it EATS you.

`What do you want?' I said.

`May I borrow a – uh . . .' She paused as if she was trying to

remember something. `The sticky stuff, Har-Har.'

`What are you waffling about?' I snapped. `What sticky stuff?'

`That,' she said, pointing over my shoulder.

I glanced back at my desk. 'Tape?'

'Thank you,' said Esha.

'I haven't said you can have it yet,' I said. I folded my arms across my chest. 'What do you need tape for? You're not inventing, are you? Because you're BANNED, remember?'

'Not inventing, Har-Har-Har,' said Esha. 'I have more important work, Har-Har-Har.'

I blinked. 'More important than inventing?'

'Precisely, Har-Har.'

Beside me, Berty looked up at Esha and growled again.

Without a word, I went back to my desk, picked up the tape and handed it over.

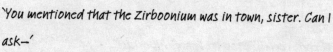

'Most grateful,' said Esha. She blinked at me slowly. 'You mentioned that the Zirboonium was in town, sister. Can I ask—'

'Zirboonium?' I rolled my eyes. 'How many times, Esha? I don't want to hear about that stupid rock!'

'A stupid rock, it is not,' she said with a frown. 'No, indeed. It is—'

I slammed the door in her face.

For a second there was silence, then I heard Esha going back to her room. I looked at Berty.

'Something still doesn't feel right,' I murmured.

Berty nudged my leg and snarled at the door.

'I don't know what you're saying,' I said. 'I don't speak dinosaur, do I?'

Berty blinked at me with his enormous amber eyes. I sighed and shook my head, then turned to my desk. 'I have to finish this weather report.'

Berty seized my trouser leg with his teeth.

'What are you doing?' I said. 'These are special GUM-certified trousers. Get your stinky mouth off them!'

Berty started to tug me towards the door.

'Berty!' I cried. 'Stop it! Berty! Albertus!'

Almost at once, he released my leg.

'That was bad behaviour, Albertus,' I said. 'Very bad.'

He whined and hung his head.

I looked down at my trousers. There were a few small holes where Berty's teeth had dug into them.

'Look what you did,' I said. 'You silly dinosaur! You ruined my trousers!' I opened the door and pointed to the stairs. 'Go on!

Get out! I wish Esha had never brought you here!'

Berty flinched. With an outraged squeal, he scooted towards the stairs and disappeared.

I felt a sudden pang of guilt.

'Almost there, Har-Har,' said Esha's voice, filtering out of her room. I strode towards her door, ready to tell her that she owed me a new pair of GUM trousers. 'Almost, yes. Har-Har-Har. The Ma and The Pa will be proud of you, Goospa.'

The Ma and The Pa?

Goospa?

Quietly, I placed my ear against her door.

'Nobody else will have thought to gift them a planet, Har-Har. What a planet, too! The planet of the Earthly blue-berry. Better

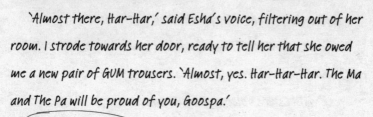

than anything a worm-weed crown princess would come up with. They will be pleased, yes. Most pleased. Soon, The Ma and The Pa will see their mistake. Zelpha shall have a crown prince instead of a crown princess.'

Zelpha?

I frowned. It seemed ridiculous, but what if . . . what if Esha had been telling the truth? What if she had been replaced by a shapeshifting alien from a planet called Zelpha? And what if she really was stranded on Planet 403 like she'd said?

[A note from Esha: I am surprised Nishi's brain didn't **EXPLODE** from this lightbulb moment.]

'Well, there's one way to find out,' I murmured.

I took a deep breath; then I knocked on the door.

There was a low scuffling sound, like something being quickly put away.

'Yes?' said Esha's voice a moment later.

'Hey, Esha!' I said, opening the door. She was sitting at her desk, a peculiar smile on her face.

'Yes, dear sister?' she said. There was an impatient edge to her voice. 'Was there something you require? Or perhaps you have remembered where one would acquire the Zirboonium?'

'I – uh . . .' I stared at her closely. Whatever-that-was-in-the-chair looked exactly like Esha. 'I was just wondering. Do you remember that time we went cloud-spotting together?' I asked.

Esha thought for a moment. 'Cloud-spotting, Har-Har-Har. Why, yes. Lots of fun. Har-Har-Har.'

'We should do it again sometime,' I said quietly.

'Yes, Har-Har-Har,' said Esha. 'Most certainly. Har-Har-Har.'

I could still hear her strange laugh as I shut the door. I hurried back to my room and sat down on my bed, breathing shakily.

NO WONDER Berty had been acting so strangely.

That wasn't Esha.
That was an IMPOSTER!

Esha had never been cloud-spotting with me in my **ENTIRE LIFE**. Not even when I'd tried to bribe her with my pocket money.

'This is terrible,' I murmured. 'I should have listened to Esha. ~~My brilliant, amazing, genius sister was right all along.'~~

[A note from Nishi: Esha, I did NOT say this. STOP interfering in my story!]

I stared at my bedroom door. Just a few paces away, there was a shapeshifting alien sitting in Esha's bedroom.

I couldn't believe she'd let something like this happen.

What a complete **NINCOMPOOP**.

I drummed my fingers on my lap, trying to remember what Esha had said over the talkie. Something about the alien wanting to teleport Earth. I had to stop that from happening. Only I had no idea how. I couldn't exactly tell Mum or Dad. They'd never believe me. And I couldn't let Alien Esha know that I suspected her. I had to play it cool.

[A note from Esha: I have informed Nishi that she could not be cool if she was stranded in a snowstorm.]

I had to try and contact Esha.

I darted towards my desk and picked up the talkie, swivelling the dial. 'Come on, come on,' I said, but it stayed silent. For one terrible moment, I wondered if the reason Esha wasn't answering was because she couldn't. What if . . . ? No. I pushed the thought out of my mind.

Esha might have been the MOST annoying sister ever, but ~~she was smart~~ she'd grown up with a brilliant sister like me. I knew she'd be able to look after herself.

What I needed was a plan.

'OK, Nishi,' I said. 'First things first. What do you know about this alien? One – it can shapeshift. Two – it's from a planet

called Zelpha. Three – it's trying to build some kind of device to teleport Earth. Four – it keeps asking about Zirboonium. Five – it needs to be stopped immediately.'

Well, that wasn't much help.

After all, I didn't have any alien-stopping technology in my room.

[A note from Esha: Nishi had forgotten about her stinky wellingtons. I am quite sure they could knock out an entire alien ARMY.]

I sat down on my bed again and stared at the door. Whatever I was going to do, I had to figure it out QUICKLY.

When Is a Volcano Not a Volcano?

'Archie?' whispered Broccoli for the THOUSANDTH time.

We had been walking for a while. The air felt icier than before and the sky around us had started to change colour, transforming into a menacing shade of grey.

'How much further?' grumbled Bean ahead of us. He and Broccoli hadn't spoken since their argument. Once or twice, I'd caught Bean glancing back at Broccoli and Archibald as if he wanted to say something, but each time he'd turn around and continue walking. 'My feet hurt. Actually, I can't even feel my feet any more because it's so cold.'

For once, he was right.

It was FREEZING.

My fingers were cold, my toes were cold and my breath formed circles in front of me as we trudged forward. To make everything worse, I still had a horrible feeling in the bottom of my stomach. I couldn't stop thinking about my family and how I had treated them. Like a total DRONG.

I'd tried distracting myself by thinking about other things; I'd even tried to make a list of all the amazing inventions I would make when I returned home. But it hadn't helped. I couldn't make it go away.

'I think I've got frostbite in my fingers,' whined Bean.

'Quite possibly,' said Nix sourly. 'Night will be falling soon. We must find my ship before then or else we will freeze to death and never get off this planet. The Earth will be teleported, the galaxy destroyed—'

'My toes feel like they're about to drop off.'

'Pity it is not your tongue,' said Nix. 'Now be quiet.'

'Wait, what are those things?' said Bean. He pointed to a series of **ENORMOUS CRATERS** bulging out of the ground a short distance ahead of us. There must have been at least twenty of them, each one rising out of the purple rock like an angry boil. 'They look like volcanoes. Are they volcanoes? I bet they're volcanoes,' he said.

'No, nada, **no**' said Nix. There was a new edge to her voice. It was the same kind of voice Mum used when she was worried about something but didn't want us to know about it. 'They are **not** volcanoes.'

She checked her tracker, looked up at the sky, then at the craters again, a nervous expression on her face.

As we got closer, I cast my genius eye over the craters. It was just **MORE** purple rock. Why would Nix be **worried** about that?

'What are they then?' asked Bean. 'I still think they're volcanoes.'

'Hurry, Earthlings.' She sped forward, still glancing uneasily at the craters. 'We are running out of time. And . . . stay *quiet*.'

'Esha, Archie still hasn't woken up,' said Broccoli, trotting beside me. He sniffed miserably. 'Maybe he's in a coma. I have to get him to a vet before it's too late.' He checked his watch. 'It's 2.30 p.m. We've only got an hour left until The Optimum Time. If we don't get back soon, there might not *be* an Earth – **or ANY VETS!**'

I was wondering if I should finally point out that Broccoli's EVIL tortoise was *only acting* when Nix suddenly began to RUN.

'This is it, Earthlings,' she said excitedly. 'This is where my ship should be.' She disappeared around a crater. 'At last, we can—'

She came to a sudden halt, her voice **trail**ing off. We stopped beside her, panting heavily as we saw . . .

. . . a great, grand

NOTHING.

In all directions there was only **more** purple rock, **more** craters and ZERO ships.

'Where is it then?' said Bean. 'I can't see a ship.'

Nix jabbed her tracker. 'It does not make sense. According to my readings, it should be here.'

Bean snorted. **'BOR-ING.** You made us walk all this way and you don't even have a ship.'

'Maybe your readings are *wrong*,' I said coolly, feeling just a teensy-tiny bit pleased that she'd messed up.

Nix turned on the spot, the tracker held out in front of her. 'It *has* to be here.'

Bean took out his slingshot and stalked off. 'I'm going to find something *interesting* to do. Without you **bore-brains.'**

I glanced at Broccoli, who opened his mouth, then shut it again.

'Is that a good idea?' I said. 'Letting Bean go off like that? You know what he's like.'

Broccoli shrugged. 'He can do what he wants. I don't care any more.' He stroked Archibald's shell gently. 'I'm going to get you back to Earth, Archie. I *promise*. As soon as we locate the ship amongst all these craters . . .'

'The craters . . .' murmured Nix. She checked her tracker again. 'PLAGUE OF THE SOLAR WINDS!' Without another word, she raced off towards the crater in front of us.

'Where are you going?' I said, hurrying after her. 'Nix?'

Broccoli glanced in the direction of Bean, who was heading for another crater opposite, then he sped after me. 'Wait – I'm coming too.'

Holding her tracker out in front of her, Nix clambered to the top of the crater.

'There it is,' she whispered, peering over the edge. 'You see, Earthlings. I told you it was here. It must have fallen in. That's why we could not see it.' She shook her head. 'That dung-drop Goospa. Wait till I find him. He will be sorry.'

I scrabbled after her, slipping and sliding across the uneven rock as I pulled myself up onto the top.

Leaning forward, I looked over the edge of the crater. It stretched downwards for miles. In the gloom, a LONG way from where we were standing, was a large object. It looked like a giant lemon and was precariously balanced on a bulge of rock. Across the side, in shiny silver, were the letters

KOOPLARZA.

'Thank the stars for the **emergency shield**,' said Nix. 'The ship appears undamaged. Now to retrieve it.'

Out of the corner of my eye, I spotted Archibald sneak a curious glance into the crater. Then he shut his eyes again.

Only this time, he wasn't quite quick enough.

'Archie?' said Broccoli. He held him up to his face. 'You just opened your eyes!'

Archibald made a noise that sounded like, 'Bother!' and opened his eyes properly.

'Esha, look!' Broccoli's snot shook with delight. **'Archie's awake!'**

'I can see that,' I said, narrowing my eyes at his **EVIL** tortoise.

'How are you feeling, Archibald? I'm sorry I left you on that buggy with Bean.' He touched his finger to Archibald's claw. 'I don't know why I was so excited about having a brother, Archie. A tortoise is just as good. Better, actually.'

Archibald gave me a smug smirk.

EURGH.

Beside me, Nix was looking
worriedly at the sky, which had
become even darker. The flashes of
green and silver light, which had been
above us all day, were slowly disappearing into the gloom.

'The night is almost upon us.' She cast another anxious
look around the craters. 'We must get my ship before the
vilter awakens.'

'Vilter?' said Broccoli. 'What's that?'

'Do you remember what I told you about this planet,
Earthling?' said Nix, her voice a low whisper. 'About there
being something much worse here than Ice Bats and
lava marshes? About a creature you should *hope* we

NEVER
ENCOUNTER?'

Broccoli nodded, eyes wide.

'The vilter is that creature.' Nix shuddered.
'When **night falls**, it shall surface to hunt. In the
day it stays underground, **DEEP** inside these craters.
Sleeping. Hiding from the light.

As long as it remains asleep, we will be safe. If it wakes, we shall be **gobbled**. Do you understand?

➤ **CRUNCHED-**

SNAP-

CRACK-

SNAP!'

Broccoli gulped and glanced above us. 'But it's **almost dark** already,' he said.

'That is why we must get down there at once,' said Nix. 'We can climb down and retrieve my ship before the *foul beast* wakes up. But we must be quiet.'

'**WAHOOOOOOOO!**' echoed a voice behind us.

We whirled round. Bean was leaning into another crater, his hands cupped around his mouth.

'**WAHOOOOOOO!**' he shouted again. The noise rolled around the crater then echoed back towards us, ear-splittingly **LOUD.**

'**WAHOOOO! WAHOOOOOOO!**'

'Curse of The Nightly Nebulas,' spat Nix.

'That fool is going to **WAKE** the vilter.'

'It can't be worse than a Guzzler,' I said airily.

'Or **DINOSAURS.** Because we've faced both—'

'WAHOOOOOOO! CHECK OUT THIS

IT'S AWESOME!'

I watched, as if in slow motion, as Bean slid his slingshot out of his pocket.

Nix gasped. 'What – is he – doing?'

Before either of us could move, she began to run towards Bean, leaping down the side of the crater with impressive speed.

Broccoli and I sprinted down after her.

'Desist, Earthling!' hissed Nix as she ran. Bean glanced back over his shoulder, frowning as he caught sight of us racing towards him.

'**DO NOT USE** that foolish contraption!'

Bean looked down at his slingshot, then back at Nix. A wicked grin spread over his face. With lightning-quick speed, he slipped a marshmallow inside it – and fired it **INTO THE CRATER.**

BLOP!

The marshmallow rocketed into the crater.

BLOP! BLOP! BLOP!

'HAHA!' said Bean, watching with glee. 'LOOK AT IT GO! That's totally—'

TA-DUM!

I stopped mid-run.

TA-DUM!

I could feel the rock beneath me

VIBRATING

with movement.

The movement of something **BIG.**

'What is that?' gasped Broccoli.

'WOAH!' Bean's arms spun in the air as he **wobbled** dangerously over the edge of the crater.

TA-DUM!

TA-DUM!

The ground was shuddering faster now, so fast that **HUGE** clouds of purple dust shot into the air around us.

TA-DUM!

TA-DUM!

'Trouble of The Tuffy Terras!' whispered Nix. 'I told you to desist!'

All of a sudden, the shuddering **stopped.** I glanced at the ground, then at Broccoli, whose snot was glittering with purple specks.

'It's stopped,' I murmured, breathing a sigh of relief.

PHEW!

Nix wiped the dust off her face and marched towards Bean. 'You foolish—'

TA-DUM!

The ground  with **SUCH FORCE** that I was thrown off my feet into the air.

225

TA-DUM!

I sat up with a loud groan. Ahead of me, Broccoli was sitting up too. He looked positively **DIZZY.**

TA-DUM! TA-DUM!

Something was very definitely coming **UP**

OUT OF THE CRATER.

'BEAN, GET AWAY FROM THERE!' Broccoli shouted. He **wobbled** to his feet, clutching Archie. 'It's not safe!'

'I DON'T NEED YOU TO TELL ME WHAT TO DO, **BORE-BRAIN!**' retorted Bean. He put his hands on his hips and glared at him. 'AND I DON'T NEED YOU TO LOOK AFTER ME, SO YOU CAN STOP TRYING, OK?'

Before Broccoli could reply, something **SHOT** OUT of the crater.

How Not to Fight a Vilter

I stared in **horror** as the creature **unfurled** itself in front of us, TOWERING into the grey sky.

Now, I know what you're thinking, Reader. You are thinking that a **genius inventor** who has encountered dinosaurs, Guzzlers and **weathernovas** can't possibly be afraid of anything – BUT that's probably because you have never encountered a vilter before.

[A note from Broccoli: Personally, I would have been quite happy never to have met one either.]

The vilter was built like an **ENORMOUS** cobra snake. It had shiny green scales, which rippled dangerously as it slid further into the air. The top of its head and the hood around its neck shimmered a fiery orange colour. Dangling under its neck was a scaly pouch. Its eyes gleamed a cold, icy blue and were positioned vertically on its head, one below the other. Between its eyes was its MOUTH. A red, **forked tongue** slid in and out as it looked down at us.

'VILTER!'

yelled Nix. She sped back in the opposite direction and threw herself behind another crater. 'Hide, Earthlings! Hide or be eaten!'

The vilter hissed, its tongue sliding in and out.

At the edge of the crater, looking like a teensy-tiny easy-to-squish human BLOB, was Bean. He teetered on the edge, gazing up at the terrifying beast.

'BEAN!' roared Broccoli. He sprinted forward, his feet hardly touching the ground as he raced towards the crater. 'GET AWAY FROM THERE!'

The vilter's head flitted towards my apprentice and its eyes NARROWED further.

Bean didn't move.

'BEAN! RUN! NOW!'

But Bean didn't run. Instead, he slid a marshmallow out  of his pocket and slotted it into his slingshot.

'BEAN!' I **THUNDERED,**

sprinting after Broccoli. I dug my hand into my Inventor's Kit, thinking fast. Nix had said that the vilter stayed underground to hide from the light. Bean's marshmallows weren't going to stop it, but the Glo-Pro might. **'STOP! THAT'S NEVER GOING TO—'**

BLOP!

A single marshmallow **blob** whizzed up to the vilter and **SMACKED** it in the middle of its scaly head. For one heart-stopping second, the vilter didn't move.

It lowered its head and stared at Bean without blinking. Bean stared back at it.

'BEAN, MOVE!' screamed Broccoli.

It happened in a (flash.)

The creature recoiled with a

STOMACH-CURLING

HISS.

A gleaming, *dart-like* object shot out of the pouch around its neck and *hit* Bean's arm.

With a **LOUD** shriek, he dropped his slingshot and **tumbled back** off the crater onto the rocky ground.

'**BEAN!**' shouted Broccoli.

The vilter hissed, rearing back as if it was planning to **ATTACK** again.

'Oh no you don't,' I whispered. I snapped the Glo-Pro and held it above my head like a spear. Almost at once, it began to glow, illuminating the gloomy air with a luminous yellow light.

The vilter reeled away from the brightness. With an **outraged hiss,** it

D
I
V
E
D

back inside the crater,

disappearing from view.

'Bean!' Broccoli threw himself down beside his cousin. I joined him a second later.

A sharp needle-like sting was sticking out of Bean's arm. The skin around it had turned a nasty shade of purple and was starting to swell outwards like a balloon.

Archibald poked his head out of Broccoli's pocket, his eyes **widening**.

'I don't feel so good,' murmured Bean. 'And I dropped my slingshot into that crater.'

'Out of my way, Earthling,' said Nix, pushing me aside. A **shadow** passed over her features as she looked down at Bean. 'Curse of The Free Moons,' she murmured. In one swift movement, she slipped off her blazer, wrapped it around her hand and yanked the stinger out of Bean's arm. He let out a loud shriek.

'What are you doing?' said Broccoli.

Bean whimpered softly.

'Must get it out quick,' said Nix, throwing the stinger and her blazer into the crater behind us. 'The longer you leave it, the more poison enters the body.'

'**POISON?**' I echoed.

'It hurts,' moaned Bean.

'Vilter poison,' said Nix. 'Not good. No, **nada, no.** Works fast. Eats you up from the inside. If he is not treated . . .' She trailed off, leaving the thought hanging in the air between us like a storm cloud.

Broccoli swallowed. 'What can we do? We have to **help** him.'

'I have a medical kit on my ship,' said Nix. 'Zelpha-standard. It contains an anti-poison.' She frowned. 'But we only have FIFTEEN EARTHLING MINUTES to administer it. After that, it will be too late.'

'Fifteen minutes?' I echoed. 'But your ship's at the bottom of that crater!'

'Then we move quickly,' said Broccoli firmly. He glanced at the sky, then at the crater behind us. 'It's nearly **dark**. Will the vilter come out again?'

'It will surface eventually to hunt for food,' said Nix, 'but it will stay away from that.' She nodded at the Glo-Pro. 'How long will the light last?'

'I don't know,' I admitted. 'It's only the second prototype.'

(I didn't tell her that the first prototype had stopped working after exactly two minutes and fifty-five seconds.)

Bean whimpered again.

'I'm going to fix this, Bean,' said Broccoli. 'We're going to make you better. Isn't that right, Esha?'

I nodded furiously. 'Absolutely. We're the best genius inventor-apprentice duo across all the galaxies,

THE TEAM OF DREAMS.

remember? We're not going to let anything happen to you, Bean. Imagine what your parents would say!'

He smiled weakly. 'I'm sorry for not listening to you, James,' he said. 'I should've moved away when you said.'

SORRY...

Broccoli blinked at Bean in surprise, then squeezed his hand. 'I'm sorry about your slingshot. We'll get you

I'M SORRY

another one. Help me get him up, Esha.'

Carefully, he placed Bean's arm around his neck. 'Come on, Bean. We're just going to walk to that crater there,' he said as we lifted him to his feet.

'I'm not sure I can,' whispered Bean, his face worryingly pale.

'Course you can,' said Broccoli. He forced a smile onto his face. 'You're the slingshot supremo, remember. You can do anything. It's not as far as it looks. Trust me. One step at a time. Quick as you can.'

'What about the creature?' whispered Bean, wincing as he walked.

234

'Don't worry about that,' said Broccoli. 'It won't come near us while we've got the Glo-Pro.'

'Where were you?' I said to Nix. She strode along beside me, her gaze flitting warily between the craters. 'You could have helped us instead of **hiding**.'

'You **cannot** fight a vilter,' said Nix.

'I did,' I said, and waved the Glo-Pro at her.

'And I won.'

Nix frowned. 'You were lucky, Earthling,' she said, but I was quite sure she looked a teensy-tiny bit ashamed.

We reached the edge of the crater and peered inside.

'You see, Bean?' said Broccoli. 'There's the ship right there. We go down and we get that anti-poison.

Easy-peasy.'

Easy-peasy wasn't quite how I would have described it. But at least there was no sign of the vilter. **Yet.**

'What if it comes up while we're trying to get the ship?' I asked.

'Then we are **DOOMED,**' said Nix, her face pinched with **worry**.

(So much for being positive.)

'But we have no choice. It is the only way to reach the ship.'

'I can't climb down there,' said Bean. His face was shining with sweat.

'He is correct,' said Nix. 'He is too weak.'

'We'll wait here, Bean,' said Broccoli gently, helping him sit on the rock. 'Esha and Nix will go down and fly the ship up to us.'

I stared at the rock and wished, *more than anything,* that I had my **jelly-powered backpack** with me. It would have been **MUCH** easier to fly down to the ship rather than climb.

[A note from Broccoli: I have reminded Esha that the jetpack would have been a bad idea anyway, considering the first prototype melted.]

'We must climb carefully,' said Nix. 'If we **fall**, we will be –' she slapped one hand against the other –

'CRUSHED– MUSHED– SQUISHED.

If we make a **sound**, we will alert the vilter and be

CRUSHED– MUSHED– SQUISHED.

If we—'

'I understand,' I said quickly.

'I shall go first,' said Nix. 'Follow me and *move quickly*. We must be in and out before the vilter discovers us. Your friend doesn't have long.'

I tried to ignore the **wobbly** feeling in my stomach as she disappeared into the crater.

'We'll have the ship up here before you know it, Bean. The vilter doesn't stand a chance.' I glanced at the Glo-Pro; then I pushed it into Broccoli's hand. 'Here, take this.'

'What about you?' said Broccoli. 'If you give it to us, you'll have **nothing** to protect you in the crater.'

'Don't be ridiculous, Broccoli,' I said, hoping I sounded braver than I felt. 'I have my genius, remember? I don't need a Glo-Pro.'

'But—'

'I'll be fine. Just don't get **EATEN** while I'm down there.'

Forcing a smile onto my face, I threw him a wave, then lowered myself down into the crater.

The Marvel of Marmalade
[written mostly by Broccoli]

'Bean,' I whispered, once Nix and Esha had disappeared into the crater.

I'd helped him lie down on the rock. His eyes were closed, his breath coming sharp and fast. I touched his arm. His skin was burning. 'Bean?' He groaned softly and opened his eyes.

'Is the ship here yet?' he whispered.

'Not yet, Bean. Don't worry, they won't be long. I know Esha. She'll make sure we get you on that ship in time.'

He nodded weakly and shut his eyes again.

I checked my watch. We only had eleven minutes left to administer the anti-poison. Archibald poked his head out of my pocket and put his claw on my hand.

'I know, Archie,' I murmured under my breath. 'We need that anti-poison FAST.'

Above us the sky had completely darkened into a thick gloom. The only light came from the Glo-Pro, which shone softly. I shivered. My fingers were cold, my ears were frozen and my nose was numb. I wished I had a Snot Scarf with me.

More than anything, I wished that we were on Earth instead of being stranded on this silly planet.

I checked my watch again.

Come on, Esha.

Suddenly a nose-twitching HISS echoed through the air.

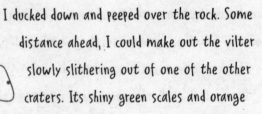

I ducked down and peeped over the rock. Some distance ahead, I could make out the vilter slowly slithering out of one of the other craters. Its shiny green scales and orange hood shimmered eerily in the gloom.

It paused, its head moving one way then another as if it was scanning the purple rock. I gulped.

Nix had been right. It had come back up for food.

That meant us.

I glanced at Bean. If the vilter spotted us, he didn't stand a chance. I shoved the Glo-Pro in my pocket so that we wouldn't attract the vilter's attention. Then I dragged Bean further along the side of the rocky crater, doing my best to keep him hidden. He moaned softly.

Suddenly I stumbled. I looked down. Under my shoe there

was a gap in the rock – a narrow, jagged crack, which widened gradually as it ran up across the crater. A crack that looked just big enough to hide Bean inside.

I rolled him carefully into the gap. His arm was even more swollen now, the skin almost the same colour as a plum.

The vilter HISSED again, the sound making my nose tremble.

Bean opened his eyes. 'Is that the creature? Has it come back out?'

I hesitated.

'Broccoli?'

'Well – yes – but there's nothing to worry about,' I said. 'It doesn't know where we are.'

'It doesn't?'

'Here.' I pushed the Glo-Pro into his hand. 'Keep hold of this. I'm going to check on it.'

'Don't leave me,' Bean said. 'Please.'

'I'll be back in a second. I just want to see where it is. You don't need to be scared, OK? You're not on your own.' Carefully, I lifted Archibald out of my pocket and placed him beside Bean. 'Archie's going to be right here with you. Isn't that right, Archie?'

Archibald looked me in the eye for a moment, then he touched a claw to Bean's cheek.

'Thanks, Archie,' I whispered. 'Now, stay quiet.'

Trying to make as little noise as possible, I wriggled up to the top of the crater and peered over the edge. I could see the vilter combing the purple rock, its scales gleaming as it moved through the gloom. It was close enough for me to see its tongue flicking in and out, searching. Searching for US.

 I had to (WARN) Esha and Nix.

'Esha,' I whispered into the crater. 'Esha, the vilter's come back OUT.'

No response.

'Esha?' I said again, slightly louder this time. 'Nix? The vilter's OUTSIDE.'

Still nothing.

I sniffed. Esha and Nix had to be ready to bring the ship out any minute now. If I could find a way to distract the vilter, it would buy them time to fly out safely. The Glo-Pro would hopefully make sure I didn't get eaten in the process.

I scrabbled back down the rock towards Bean.

'Is everything OK?' he murmured.

'Everything's great,' I said, smiling weakly.

Archibald blinked at me in concern.

[A note from Esha: I am quite sure that Broccoli's tortoise doesn't have a CONCERNED bone in his entire reptilian body.]

'What about Esha and Nix? Have they got the ship out?'

'Er - not yet,' I said, peeping over the rock. The vilter was still scanning the craters.

'Do you think we'll make it back in time?' whispered Bean. His voice wobbled. 'I don't want Earth to be teleported and I don't want the galaxy to be destroyed. I want to go home.'

'We will,' I said firmly. 'We're going to stop Goospa, Bean. As soon as we've got you the anti-poison.' I eased the Glo-Pro out of his hand. 'I'm just going to borrow this for a second.'

'What are you doing?' said Bean.

'Stay quiet, OK?'

Just then, the Glo-Pro flickered.

'Oh, no, not now. Please,' I whispered.

The Glo-Pro flashed again, then went dark.

'Come on,' I hissed, giving it a shake.

Nothing happened.

My nose twitched furiously. Without the Glo-Pro, I didn't stand a chance.

Fingers trembling, I checked my pockets for anything that might help me.

Tissues - no.

Notebook - no.

Nose peg - no.

More tissues - no.

Bottle of Orange Marmalade Spray - wait.

I stared at it. Chapter 41 of the *Inventor's Handbook* said that *the best inventors can find a solution even in the trickiest of situations*. But I didn't see how a bottle of Marmalade Spray could help me with a vilter.

BANG!

A tremendous noise sounded from the crater.

Esha!

They must be bringing the ship up.

The vilter had heard it too. Its head darted towards the crater. With a loud hiss, it began to slither in our direction.

Oh dear.

Bean's eyes widened.

'Broccoli?' he said in a small voice. 'Is it coming?'

I shook my head. 'I told you, Bean. I'm going to keep you safe.'

'How? The Glo-Pro isn't working. You can't fight it with marmalade.'

I stared at the Glo-Pro for a long second; then I looked at the bottle of Marmalade Spray, the beginnings of an idea sprouting in my brain. 'Or maybe I can,' I murmured.

'How?' said Bean, as I gave the bottle of marmalade a hard shake.

'Do you know what happens when you drop Marmalade Spray into a Glo-Pro?' I said.

Archibald's eyes widened.

'You almost send a shed into outer space, that's what.'

I peeped over the rim of the crater again. The vilter was moving faster now, its body shimmying across the ground with breathtaking speed. I ducked back down and glanced at the Glo-Pro and the liquid marmalade.

This was either going to be a VERY BAD idea or COMPLETELY GENIUS.

[A note from Esha: I have since informed Broccoli that at times it is difficult to know the difference between the two.]

'Look after him, Archie,' I said.

'Broccoli?' said Bean. 'What are you doing?'

I took a deep breath, looked at Archibald (who gave me a reassuring smile), then, clutching both the marmalade and the Glo-Pro, I climbed onto the top of the crater and waved at the vilter.

'HEY THERE!' I bellowed as loudly as I could.

'HALLOOOOOOOOOOO!'

The vilter stopped in its tracks, close enough for me to see its gleaming blue eyes. Eyes fixed directly on me.

'YES, YOU!' I shouted, trying to hide the shake in my voice. 'I'M TALKING TO YOU! YOU WANT TO EAT ME, DON'T YOU? WELL COME ON THEN! I'M THE TASTIEST MEAL YOU'RE EVER GOING TO GET, BUT YOU'LL HAVE TO CATCH ME FIRST!' I slid off the crater and began backing away in the opposite direction. 'COME ON! COME AND GET ME!'

With an enraged HISS, the vilter changed direction and began moving towards me.

Ignoring the twitchy itch in my nose, I turned and ran. Across the rock I went, looping and twisting between the craters. The

ground shook as the vilter raced after me, making a noise like an angry kettle. I glanced back over my shoulder and immediately wished I hadn't. The vilter was much closer than I'd realized.

Its scales glinted.

Its eyes drilled into mine, cold and empty.

A sting shot out of the pouch around its neck and landed a short distance behind me.

I sprinted faster, dust flying into the air as I pounded across the ground.

HISS!

Another stinger landed behind me. Too close.

I sped forward, heading for the furthest crater.

Another stinger whizzed through the air. I heard its loud ZIP as I dived out of its way.

'BROCCOLI!'

I looked back at the sound of my name, my mouth dropping.

Bean had somehow climbed to the top of the crater and was kneeling on top of it.

'BROCCOLI! WHAT ARE YOU DOING?'

'BEAN, GET DOWN FROM THERE!' I shouted. Too late.

The vilter had seen him too. It slowed, its head swivelling towards him.

Time for the ULTIMATE DISTRACTION.

Panting, I pulled the lid off the Glo-Pro and emptied the entire contents of the Orange Marmalade Spray inside.

I stuck the lid back on and shook it, hard. The Glo-Pro **fizzed and popped**, glimmering a brilliant SHINY orange.

'HEY!' I bellowed at the vilter. 'OVER HERE, YOU OVERSIZED WORM!'

It looked at me with irritation, its tongue flicking in and out.

I stretched my arm back; then I threw the fizz-popping Glo-Pro towards it.

It flew through the air, a MARVELLOUS MARMALADE MISSILE, and . . .

disappeared directly into the vilter's OPEN MOUTH.

<u>AH</u>.

That wasn't (exactly) what I'd planned.

The vilter's tongue flicked in and out as it glared at me.

I stepped back, my nose twitching.

'BROCCOLI, RUN!' yelled Bean.

The vilter glanced between us as if it was trying to decide which one of us to eat first. Its tongue flicked in and out again. Then, with a stomach-churning SNARL, it slid towards me.

Inside the Crater

In case you, the Reader, are wondering,
climbing down a crater is **EXTREMELY** difficult.
It is **EVEN MORE DIFFICULT** when you:

1. Do not have any rope, a jetpack or safety gear.
2. Might be discovered by a **GIANT** cobra lookalike
   monster at any minute.
3. Are an inventor, **NOT** a world-class climber.

My feet scrabbled against the rock as I searched for
a hold.

'Watch it, Earthling!' hissed Nix from below, as a few
pebbles **bounced** off the rock towards her.

Taking a deep breath, I inched myself downwards.
Any moment now, I was quite certain that the vilter would
appear below us and we'd be **CRUSHED - MUSHED -
SQUISHED** before we'd even reached the ship.

'Hurry up, Earthling,' whispered Nix, her voice echoing
around the rock.

'I'm trying,' I said, through gritted teeth. My arms and legs were aching and the back of my neck was soaked with sweat. My trainers were absolutely NOT designed for crater climbing. Instead of gripping to the rock, they kept slipping and sliding across it. As if all that wasn't bad enough, the crater **STANK** of rotten onions and **mouldy-oldy cheese**. The STINK was so bad that it was making my head hurt.

'How much further?' I panted, gagging a little as the stink floated into my mouth.

'Keep going,' said Nix unhelpfully.

We must have been about halfway down when I thought I heard a voice above me. A faint whisper, calling my name.

I looked up, but all I could see above me was the night sky.

'Broccoli?' I whispered. 'Is that you?'

No reply.

'Nix, did you hear that?'

'Stop talking, keep moving,' said Nix.

I craned my head upwards, but there was nothing. Maybe this stink was making me imagine things. But that didn't explain why my inventor's instincts were tingling like mad. And I still couldn't shake the feeling that I *had* heard something. Maybe Broccoli was in trouble. Maybe they needed help up there.

We *had* to get to the ship.

Ignoring my achy arms and legs, I inched down as fast as I could.

Nix skimmed over the final section of rock and hopped down onto the ship with a

(((**LOUD BANG**.)))

It teetered unsteadily. She marched over the letters **KOOPLARZA** towards the front.

'Cosmic calamities,' she muttered. 'The door is stuck!'

'What do you mean – stuck?' I puffed.

The ship creaked dangerously as Nix wrestled with the handle. I slid down the last section of rock and leapt onto the ship after Nix. It groaned a little more under both our weight, wavering. A few loose pebbles skittered off the rock and disappeared into the gloom below.

'Stay there!' she snapped.

'Or you will send us to the bottom!'

The KOOPLARZA rattled as she finally yanked the door open and slipped inside, leaving me on the far end of the ship.

Seconds passed. I chewed my lip. What was she doing in there?

'Nix?' I hissed.

There was a muffled reply.

'Nix!' I whispered fiercely. 'We have to get this ship up there now! Bean needs that anti-poison!'

No reply.

'Right, that's it,' I muttered. I'd had enough of waiting around for Nix. I could help with whatever she was doing in there. After all, I was a genius inventor. Slowly, I edged towards the open door.

The ship creaked again.

I paused, trying very hard not to think of the COLOSSAL drop below.

I took another step forward.

The ship wobbled dangerously beneath me, but the door was only a few steps away now.

I took another teensy-tiny step forward.

The ship tilted again—

I leapt towards the open door, my arms **SLAMMING** painfully against the metal as I grabbed the edge.

Only I didn't grab it. Instead, my fingers (already tired from all that PESKY climbing) slipped. I **bounced** off the edge of the ship and . . .

F
E
L
L into the crater.

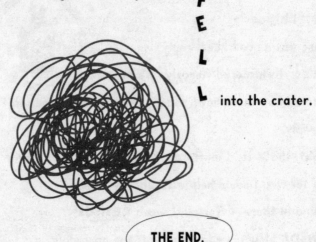

THE END.

[A note from Broccoli: Do not be alarmed, Reader. This is not the moment where Esha Verma, genius inventor, becomes a genius splat. As usual, Esha is just being a little dramatic.]

OK, well *almost* THE END.

Air whooshed past my face and **THUNDERED** in my ears as I plummeted into the gloom. My eyes blinked at triple speed; my stomach twisted; the button on my dungarees flapped open (I had, of course, forgotten to close it), and out fell my Inventor's Kit including but not limited to:

1. My last reserve orange.
2. A ruler.
3. The list of all my hidden prototypes (in case I forgot their location).
4. A toy duck.
5. A ball of string.
6. Two pairs of sunglasses.
7. Five corks.
8. Three hairbands.
9. A bag of dried flowers.
10. A back-up list of all my hidden prototypes (in case I lost the first one).

11. Half a paratha.
12. Four keys.
13. Three spare socks.
14. One jalebi.
15. One floppy mop head.
16. A spare button.

I am sure that you, the Reader, are probably wondering why I didn't use these things to make a **BRILLIANT** invention to save myself, but I was too busy **FALLING** to think straight.

The crater flashed past me as I zoomed downwards. And I knew, with 100% certainty, that this was **IT.** ←

I had escaped dinosaurs, Guzzlers and a **weathernova**, only to be squished inside a **rotten** crater on a **rotten** planet, and really the whole thing just seemed **SO UNFAIR** when—

THRUM!

Suddenly, the sound of an engine exploded through the air.

AN ENGINE.

I had been so busy thinking about my imminent fate that I had *forgotten* all about Nix and the ship.

 BERZING!

A loud **springy** noise echoed through the crater. A moment later, something took hold of the top of my dungarees and I stopped falling.

Something was pulling me up.

Craning my neck, I glimpsed what appeared to be an **enormous metal hook** suspended from the bottom of the ship. My stomach flipped as I flew in the opposite direction now, the crater walls whizzing past me. *Faster* and *faster*, the ship coming closer and closer until, with

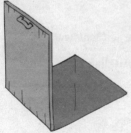

a quick flick, I was tossed inside through a trapdoor. I **tumbled** onto the floor, my whole body trembling.

'Welcome aboard KOOPLARZA, Earthling,' said Nix's voice from the front of the ship. 'I trust you had a comfortable landing.'

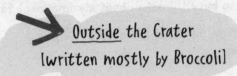

With the Glo-Pro and my only hope of survival deep inside the vilter's stomach, I did the only thing left to do.

I turned and **RAN**.

I headed towards the crater nearest to me, desperately searching for a place to hide. I imagined the vilter's blue eyes as it got closer and closer, its tongue flicking in and out and—

HISS!

I glanced back over my shoulder, certain that I was about to be CRUSHED - MUSHED - SQUISHED. But the vilter had . . . stopped.

Its face twisted. Its eyes widened. Then, without warning, its whole body started to shake. A shrill whistling noise echoed across the craters as bright orange smoke began puffing out of its ears. I watched, astonished, as it threw its head backwards. A fountain of orange smoke shot out of its mouth into the night air.

Somewhere below, I heard a deep rumbling noise. But now the vilter was doing something even more PECULIAR. It had started to slither in a circle, round and round, orange smoke still puffing out of its ears and mouth. The more it spun, the more purple dust flew into the air.

I ducked behind the crater.

Another, deeper rumble echoed through the air. Squinting through the dust, I spotted a large lemon-shaped SHIP emerging from the crater! finally!

[A note from Esha: I have pointed out to Broccoli that he should try climbing down a foul-smelling crater with no climbing equipment and see how he likes it.]

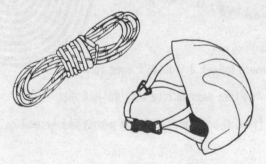

Hanging out dangerously from the door was a familiar dungarees-wearing figure. Bean, still crouching on the edge of the crater, waved. Esha gave a signal; a moment later, a long hook-like device descended from the bottom of the ship and lifted Bean into the air. As he disappeared inside, I could see him pointing in my direction.

'ESHA, I'M OVER HERE!' I yelled as she scanned the rock for me. 'ESHA!'

The vilter was still spinning, its ENORMOUS BODY BIG creating a whirlpool of purple dust so

I could barely see through it.

If I waited much longer, I wouldn't even be able to see the ship. And Esha wouldn't be able to find me!

Leaping out from the crater, I sprinted across the ground towards them.

'ESHA!' I thundered.

Suddenly she caught sight of me and waved frantically.

'BROCCOLI, WE'RE COMING!'

The ship flew closer. The vilter shrieked, its entire body enveloped in a cloud of orange and purple.

??? 'BROCCOLI, WHAT DID YOU DO?' boomed Esha's voice through the air. ???

???

'I DIDN'T DO ANYTHING!' I yelled, speeding towards her. The ship was hovering above a nearby crater, some distance away from the vilter.

'WELL, YOU MUST HAVE DONE SOMETHING!'

'IT'S NOT MY FAULT YOU TOOK SO LONG TO GET THE SHIP!' I retorted.

'WHY DON'T YOU TRY CLIMBING DOWN A CRATER WITHOUT–'

A horrible retching noise suddenly sounded behind me. Looking back, I saw the vilter's entire body swaying back and forth. The scales on its neck rippled, almost as if something was working its way up through its neck–

'BROCCOLI, MOVE!' cried Esha. 'I THINK IT'S GOING TO–'

Before I could do anything, a STREAM of sticky marmalade shot out of its mouth into the air.

SPLAP!

SPLEP!

SPLOP!

Marmalade landed either side of me. One splodge whizzed towards the ship, which veered unsteadily out of the way.

Another loud retching noise echoed through the air.

'I THINK IT'S GOING TO **BARF AGAIN!**' bellowed Esha.

This time, I didn't even look back. Panting, I scrambled up the side of the crater. The ship hovered above me, the hook-like device suspended just out of reach.

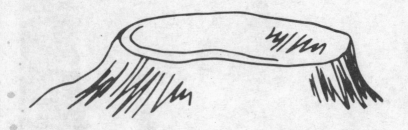

'CAN'T YOU MOVE ANY NEARER?' I hollered.

'We're getting as close as we can,' shouted Esha. 'Try and reach!'

'I am trying,' I gasped, stretching as high as I could.

'BROCCOLI, DUCK!' shouted Esha, her eyes widening as she looked at something behind me. Before I could even think about moving, a blob of marmalade landed, with a supremely sticky SPLAT, on my shoe.

'WOOAAAH!' I shouted as I lost my balance and fell forward.

'BROCCOLI, THIS IS NO TIME FOR LYING AROUND!' yelled Esha. 'MOVE!'

'I'M STUCK!' I groaned as I tried to free myself from the marmalade. My foot was held fast.

I jiggled my foot again, trying to tug it clear, but it was well and truly jammed.

[A note from Esha: I'm not sure if *jammed* is quite the right word . . . Marmaladed, maybe?]

'BROCCOLI!'

HISS!

My head shot up. Somehow, despite the fact that it was still puffing orange smoke all over the place and vomiting marmalade, the vilter was slithering towards me, its eyes filled with rage. Placing my hands around my leg, I tugged and tugged - but it was no use. I was STILL STUCK!

'Uh - *Broccoli?*' called Esha. 'Maybe take off your shoe!'

'Now you tell me!' I said, desperately pulling off the Velcro straps. The vilter was only a short distance away now. I could feel its fury rippling through the air as it surged forward.

'GOT IT!' I shouted, sliding my foot out of the shoe. I hurled myself towards the hook. This time I managed to grab it.

HISS!

Glancing over my shoulder, I saw the vilter's eyes following me as we soared upwards, away from the crater.

It retched again, then . . .

SPLAP!

SPLEP!

SPLOP!

Another **barrage** of marmalade shot

towards me as the ship roared higher into the air.

'WAAAAARRGH!' I swung around on the hook like a helpless

worm, my nostrils twitching as the marmalade splodges

whizzed past us, only just missing the ship.

'I TOLD YOU THAT MARMALADE WAS A BAD IDEA!' shouted Esha.

I opened my mouth to reply, but the wind whipped my words away.

The KOOPLARZA soared higher into the night. I looked down,

my stomach swooping as the vilter grew smaller and smaller. All

around me the sky was a syrup of gloomy darkness. The only light

came from the soft glow filtering out of the ship's trapdoor

above me.

Suddenly we STOPPED. Air whistled past my ears as the hook

began to winch me up. When I was nearly at the top, Esha grabbed

my hand and dragged me into the ship.

'Where's Bean?' I said dizzily, as I landed in a heap.

'Over here,' she said, pulling me to my feet. 'Come on. We've

only got a couple of minutes left.'

Bean was already lying on a long bunk-like apparatus that was floating in the air. Archibald was sitting on top of him, his face wrinkled in concern. Nix was busily preparing a vial of green liquid beside a sink.

'Bean?' I leaned over him.

 'Broccoli?' His arm was a deeper plum colour now and his skin had started to look scaly. His face was even more pale. 'You made it.'

'Course I did.' I sniffed, ignoring the trembling feeling in my legs. 'That vilter didn't stand a chance against my Marmalade Spray.'

Bean smiled weakly. 'I've got Archibald,' he said. He touched the top of his shell. 'Safe and sound.'

'Get out of my way!' hissed Nix. She bent over him and uncorked the vial. 'Open up,' she said to Bean.

'What is that?' murmured Bean.

'No time for questions,' she said. 'You have

less than one Earthling minute left.'

1
min

Before he could do anything, Nix forced his mouth open and poured the green liquid down his throat. Bean spluttered and groaned. His eyes flickered shut.

'BEAN?'

We all <u>stared</u> at him, including Archibald.

I held my breath. Bean wasn't moving.

Nix watched him in silence, her face grim.

'Bean?' I shook him, but there was no answer. A cold shiver ran down my spine.

'Come on, Bean,' I whispered, squeezing his hand. A horrible lump had formed in my throat. Bean might have been every kind of annoying, but he was still my cousin. My responsibility. 'Please.' A hot tear ran down my face. 'I need your help to become a big brother. I can't do it without you.'

Beside me, Esha wiped her eyes furiously.

Suddenly, Bean let out a loud gasp. A coil of green vapour rose out of his mouth into the air.

'Bean?'

He whispered something that I couldn't quite catch.

'What did you say?'

'I said - that stuff is disgusting,' he murmured, opening his eyes. 'Just like your breath, **BORE-brain.**'

How I, Nishi Verma,
~~Proved I Am a DRONG~~ Was Rudely Tricked

(told mostly by Nishi Verma)

After spending the previous hour or so running several

calculations and recalculations, I had finally devised a plan of action.

I opened my bedroom door and looked cautiously at Esha's closed door.

The door with a shapeshifting alien behind it.

I fingered the padlock in my pocket and took a deep breath.

I had a plan. Now I just had to hope it worked.

Before I could change my mind, I marched over to Esha's room and knocked on her door.

'Er — Esha?'

Again, there was a faint scuffling from inside like something being hastily dragged across the floor. Then the door opened.

'Yes, dear sister,' said the imposter Esha, in that same peculiar slow drawl. 'Can I help you?'

'I've lost my compass,' I said, pushing past her.

'Com-pass?' said Esha.

I paused in front of her cupboard. 'I think I left it in here,' I said, opening the doors and peering in.

'Is this urgent?' said Esha impatiently. 'I am quite busy.'

 'Won't be long,' I said, rummaging slowly through the top shelves. 'I was trying to keep it away from Berty. Remember how he almost ate it last month?'

'Let me help,' she said, moving beside me.

'I can look for it myself—'

'Let me help. In exchange, dear sister, you can tell me about the location of the Zirboonium.' She blinked at me expectantly.

I nodded slowly. 'Sounds fair.'

Esha beamed. 'Excellent.'

I pointed into the lower part of the cupboard, which was empty except for a mountain of smelly socks. 'Why don't you try down there?'

She bent down. I took a step back.

'This com-pass,' she said, leaning further in. 'Remind me of its appearance—'

My fingers closed on the padlock in my pocket. As she leaned forward, I pushed her inside and slammed the door. My fingers shook as I slipped the padlock across the handle and fastened it SHUT.

I breathed out.

I couldn't believe it. My plan had actually worked.

I, Nishi Verma, had just SAVED the Earth.

'What are you doing, dear sister?' said Esha. 'Let me out, Har-Har. This is not humorous.'

'You're not going anywhere,' I said, trying to make myself sound as fierce as possible. 'I know exactly what you are. You might look like Esha, but you're not. You're an alien who wants to teleport Earth. And you're not getting out of there. I've contacted the government,' I lied. 'They'll be here soon. Do you understand?'

There was a moment of silence.

Then . . .

A loud rattling began inside the cupboard. It was followed by an explosion of bright light and a series of horrible crunching noises.

The door shook.

I took a step back.

More crunching noises sounded behind the door.

Before I could do anything, the padlock flew off and the door was flung open.

A large, slimy creature in orange robes climbed out of the cupboard.

'Har-Har-Har. You did not think that would work, did you, sister of Esha-Verma-Verma-Esha? I am Goospa, the five-hundredth Prince of the Planet Zelpha, of the Triweeni Cluster in the Newporla Dimension. Exact co-ordinates: 3xyz-890-12wez. Har-Har-Har. Your Earthling tricks will not work on me.' He eyed me curiously. 'Tell me. How did you figure out I was not your sister? What gave me away?'

I stared at this creature for a long moment; then I sprinted towards the door.

'MUM!!!'

Before I could reach the door, something whipped around my arms and legs. 'OI!' I shouted, wiggling my limbs helplessly. Goospa had fashioned a lasso out of Esha's stinky sock pile and trapped me with it. 'Let go of me!'

'I think not, Har-Har-Har,' said the creature. 'I have a planet to teleport and I cannot let you, silly Earthling, get in my way.'

'Silly Earthling?' I glared at him. 'Do you even know who I am? My name is Nishi Verma and I am a GUM meteorologist!

I can name any cloud in the sky, I can spot the smallest shift in atmospheric pressure and I can predict with

80% accuracy when there's a storm coming. I am NOT scared of you.'

[A note from Esha: I am not sure why my DRONG of a sister thought any of this sounded even slightly impressive.]

'How fascinating, Har-Har,' said Goospa. He bent down and dragged something out from underneath Esha's bed. It was a circular mass of wires, twine, tape and something that looked a lot like—

'Are those dinosaur droppings?' I said, eyeing the brown blobs stuck at regular intervals along the device.

'An adequate ionic conductor,' said Goospa. 'Not the ideal, but I had no choice. Your core of Earthly supplies left much to be desired. Nevertheless, the teleporter is almost ready.'

Before I could reply, there was a low growl from the doorway. I craned my head to see Berty bursting into the room, his little legs moving like rocket thrusters.

'Help me, Berty!' I cried.

With a twirl of his arms, the creature whipped another string of stinky socks around Berty, stopping him in his tracks.

'What a foolish creature, Har-Har,' said Goospa.

Berty looked down at himself, wrapped in rainbow-coloured socks like a Christmas cracker, then whined and slumped down onto the carpet.

'Now, Earthling, you will help me,' said Goospa. 'There is one final element I need for my teleporter. Where can I find the Zirboonium?'

I stared at him. 'What? How would I know?'

'You are a terrible liar, Earthling,' said Goospa. 'I know it is here, in your town — you said so yourself. Tell me where.'

'I'm not lying,' I said. 'Maybe you should ask Esha. Shame you threw her onto another planet.'

'I do not have time for this,' said Goospa. 'It is already 2.47 p.m. on the Earthling hour. I had hoped you would tell me about the Zirboonium freely, but you have left me no choice.' He pointed at Berty. 'If you do not tell me, I will liquefy this pet of yours. You have five Earthling seconds.'

'You're bluffing,' I said. 'You can't do that. And if you think I care about that silly dinosaur, you're wrong.'

'Four.'

I glanced at Berty, who was watching me with a tragic expression on his face.

'Three.'

'I told you — I don't know!'

'Two.'

'Are you listening? I don't know!'

'I do not believe you. One. Goodbye, pet.'

'NO! WAIT!' I shouted.

Goospa paused, his head swivelling towards me.

'The Brain Trophy,' I said helplessly. 'That's what you're looking for. It's made out of Zirboonium.'

'Brain Tro-phy?' said Goospa.

'GENIE gives it every year to the best young inventor.'

'Young in-ven-tor,' Goospa said slowly. He moved across to the desk and picked up a piece of parchment. 'Har-Har — I thought I had seen something. Here it is. An invitation to the Young Inventor of the Year contest. They have even supplied a map. How kind.' He studied it closely for some moments. 'It is not far from your residence, Har-Har. The stars are in my favour.'

I glowered at him.

'Thank you, sister of Esha-Verma-Verma-Esha. You have been most helpful.'

His body shook suddenly as he transformed back into Esha.

I shuddered.

275

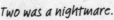

Having one sister was bad enough.

Two was a nightmare.

'The Optimum Time fast approaches — at precisely 3.30 p.m. on the Earthling hour, I shall teleport your planet.'

3.30 p.m.?

I glanced at the clock, my heart sinking.

It was almost 3 p.m. already!

He folded the map and slipped it into his pocket. 'I shall go now to this contest and retrieve the Zirboonium. My teleportation device will then be complete. At The Optimum Time, I shall teleport your planet.'

He bent and picked up the tangled ball that was his teleportation device.

'Wait!' I said as he moved towards the door. 'You're not going to get away with this! I won't let you! You might have beaten my sister, but you won't beat me! Do you understand?'

'Your threats are most amusing, Earthling. Like the rest of your species, you will be teleported. The Ma and The Pa will be most pleased with me. With the gift of your planet and its blue-berries, I, Goospa, the five-hundredth Prince of the Planet Zelpha, shall become the <u>Crown Prince</u>.' He giggled

276

in delight. 'My sister shall be Crown Princess no longer. At last, The Ma and The Pa will see that I am the worthy one. In-deed.'

'NO, wait!'

The door slammed shut behind him.

'EURGH!' I pulled against the socks around my wrists. The smell was making my head hurt. I looked down at Berty. All I could see of him was his eyes, which blinked at me sorrowfully.

'What are we going to do, Berty?'

He whined and lay down on the floor.

'Berty, you can't give up now! We have to do something.'

He shuffled around in a circle and slumped down with his back to me.

'Don't you turn your back on me, Albertus. I'm talking to you!'

[A note from Esha: If Nishi had paid any attention to my lessons on dinosaur communication, she would have known that Berty was waiting for an apology.]

277

'I don't know why you're being sulky with **me**. You should blame Esha! This is all her fault. She let that alien onto Earth in the first place. She wasn't even meant to be inventing. She's banned!'

Berty ignored me.

I glared at him.

'Fine. I don't need your help. I can stop Goospa myself.' I tugged the socks around my wrist again, trying not to breathe in their stinky fumes, but it was like trying to catch a sun ray through a nimbostratus cloud.

[A note from Esha: Apparently, this means it was VERY DIFFICULT.]

'URGH. Berty, I really need your help. Please.'

Still no response.

I groaned. I had never met a dinosaur who was so SENSITIVE in my entire life. 'Look, I'm – uh – I'm sorry for saying I wished Esha had never brought you here.'

Berty's head lifted slightly, but he stayed where he was.

'And . . . I'm sorry for not listening to you before. I know you were trying to warn me that Esha wasn't Esha, and I should have paid more attention instead of calling you a silly dinosaur. I'm **sorry**. But we need to get out of here and stop Earth being teleported. Please.'

Berty put his head back down on the carpet again.

I sighed. Trust Esha to have a T-rex as a pet. Even a goldfish would have been more—

A loud squeal of delight burst through the air. I looked up. My eyes widened. Berty's right claw had torn through the socks.

'That's it, Berty!' I exclaimed in delight. 'Go on!' ←

With a triumphant T-rex-worthy roar, he pushed another claw through the socks and pulled off the knitting around his face, threads of rainbow wool flying about in all directions.

'Berty, you clever dinosaur!' I grinned. 'Here – give me a claw, will you? We've got an alien to catch!'

'BEAN!' Broccoli pulled him into a tight hug, his snot **dancing in delight**.

'Hjajhkjshdjk,' said Bean, his voice muffled.

'What?' said Broccoli, moving away.

'I said – you're **SQUASHING ME**,' gasped Bean.

'Oh, right, sorry,' said Broccoli. He beamed. 'I'm so glad you're OK!'

Archibald bobbed his head up and down in glee and snickered as if to say, 'Well done, human worms.'

'How many times do I have to tell you, **bore-brain?**' said Bean. 'I'm the slingshot supremo. It would take more than a **No-Go planet** to take me down.'

I rubbed the top of his head. 'It's good to have you back, Bean.'

'You Earthlings,' said Nix. She was watching us with a

strange expression on her face. 'You really are peculiar. Most peculiar.' She pointed at Bean's arm. 'Swelling should go down soon.'

'Thank you, Nix,' said Bean.

'Yes, thank you, Nix,' said Broccoli.

'You SAVED his LIFE.'

'Well—' Nix cleared her throat. Then she scratched her head awkwardly, as if she wasn't quite sure what to say next.

The ship swayed sideways a little.

'Enough chitter-chatter,' said Nix, looking relieved to have a distraction. She dashed towards the console and examined a dial. 'The Optimum Time fast approaches – we have only half an Earthling hour left. I must get us to Earth so that we can stop my toad-mushroom of a brother.'

'Brother?' said Bean. 'What brother?'

'I'll explain on the way,' said Broccoli.

'Where should I land, Earthling?' said Nix, typing co-ordinates into her console.

'Home,' I said. 'That's where we left Goospa.' I gabbled my address, watching as Nix punched it in. A screen to her left *whirred* for a few moments; then it pulsed a bright yellow. A mechanical voice said, 'Co-ordinates locked.'

'Can we contact Earth now we're on your ship?' I said. 'It's just – well – I should really warn my sister. Nishi's a DRONG, but Broccoli was right. I can't leave her to deal with Goospa on her own.'

'Enter the contact sequence there,' said Nix, pointing to a numerical keypad. 'Then press the central button.'

'Contact sequence?' I blinked. 'Do you mean phone number?'

'That is what I said, Earthling,' said Nix with an impatient sigh.

I dialled Nishi's mobile number and waited, praying she would pick up.

BRING-BRING!
BRING-BRING!

The noise echoed around the ship.

'What are you going to say?' said Broccoli.

BRING-BRING!

BRING-BRING!

'Well, I—'

'Hello?'

'Nishi?'

'Esha?'

A rush of warmth flooded through me at the sound of her voice.

'Esha, is that really you?'

I took a deep breath. 'Nishi, I know you're annoyed at me about the laboratory and you're right to be – OK! **I'M SORRY.** But you really have to believe what I'm about to say. There's—'

'—a shapeshifting alien that looks like you is heading to the GENIE contest right now!'

'Wait – *what?*'

'The contest!' bellowed Nishi. 'That sneaky alien Goospa found out the **Brain Trophy** is made of Zirboonium. So he's gone to the GENIE contest, disguised as you, to steal it! Me and Berty tried to stop him, but he was too fast!' She was shouting **so loudly** that I had to take a step back from the console.

'What do you mean – you and Berty? You **hate** him! And how did Goospa find out about the trophy being made of Zirboonium? *Did you tell him?*'

'Forget about that!' said Nishi, ignoring my questions. 'WHERE ARE YOU?'

'I'm – well . . .' I glanced at Broccoli, who shrugged unhelpfully. 'It's complicated,' I said.

'Well you'd better hurry up!' squawked Nishi. 'Goospa has already left and HE STOLE MY BICYCLE!' There was a muffled sound in the distance. 'Yes, Mum, I'm coming!'

'Where are you and Mum going?' I said.

'TO THE CONTEST, OBVIOUSLY! SOMEONE HAS TO STOP HIM!'

'You're taking Mum with you?' I shouted incredulously, trying to imagine Mum and my DRONG of a sister chasing after Goospa. 'That's a **TERRIBLE** idea!'

'It's not my fault!' said Nishi. 'She thinks Goospa is you, remember? She thinks you've gone to the contest even though you're BANNED from inventing, and she's FUMING because you cycled over her begonias.'

'But that wasn't me! You have to tell her!'

'How do you expect me to do that?' retorted Nishi, her voice crackling through the console. 'If I tell her it was a shapeshifting alien, she'll think I've gone bananas!'

'GIBBONS OF THE GOLDEN GATEWAYS, CAN YOU BOTH **BE QUIET!**' cried Nix. 'I AM TRYING TO **CONCENTRATE** HERE! HAVE YOU TRIED NAVIGATING A SHIP AT A BAZILLION-KAZILLION CLICKS TO SAVE THE GALAXY, WHICH COULD BE ABOUT TO END BECAUSE OF MY BROTHER?'

There was a pause.

Then –

'YOUR

→ BROTHER?'

rumbled Nishi's voice over the console. She sounded like a volcano that was about to EXPLODE. 'YOUR **BROTHER** DID THIS?

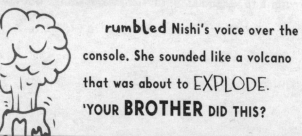

WELL, WHOEVER YOU ARE, YOU HAD BETTER GET DOWN HERE AND **FIX IT.** WE'VE GOT LESS THAN HALF AN HOUR LEFT! Yes, Mum, I'm coming! ESHA, GET TO THE GENIE CONTEST, OR ELSE.'

There was a click of a switch, then a **loud** humming noise.

'*That* is your sister?' said Nix, staring at the console in disgust.

I grinned. 'That's Nishi. You'd better put in the co-ordinates for the **GENIE** contest. It's being held at Twiddle Manor.'

'Which is **HUGE,**' said Broccoli, looking worried. 'How are we going to find Goospa?'

'He's going for the Zirboonium, so that means he'll be heading straight for the **Brain Trophy,**' I said. 'If we find the trophy, we'll find him.' I stared at each of them in grim determination. 'Get ready. We're going straight to GENIE's Half-Century Day.'

Archibald the ~~Evil~~ Hero

In case you, the Reader, are wondering, landing on Earth when you are travelling at a rate of a **bazillion-kazillion clicks** is **NOT** a pleasant experience. It is, in fact, about as pleasant as:

1. Getting your teeth pulled out by a pair of garden shears.
2. Eating a cactus.
3. Falling into a hive of bees.

Landing on Earth when you are travelling at a rate of a bazillion-kazillion clicks is also very *difficult*. It is so difficult that, despite some expert flying from Nix, the **KOOPLARZA SQUASHED** an entire row of metal railings, bent three trees and shaved the tails off a family of unsuspecting squirrels.

It was quite the entrance.

'Here we are,' declared Nix as the ship **juddered** to a screeching halt. 'This is the location you gave me, Earthling.'

I peeled myself out from under the chair beside her and **wobbled** to my feet. There, through the ship's screen, glittering in the afternoon sunlight, was ...EARTH. Beautiful, brilliant Earth. I grinned, my heart swelling with SPINGLY-TINGLY delight. I had never thought I'd be as **happy** to see my home planet as I was at that particular moment.

'We're here,' breathed Broccoli. He high-fived Bean and picked up Archibald, dancing with him in the air. 'Look at that, Archie! We made it back from Planet 403!'

For the first time in his reptilian life, Archibald didn't seem disappointed. Instead, he waggled his claws in a peculiar kind of tortoise dance, his head **bobbing** in glee.

(I suppose even an EVIL reptile can get tired of seeing the same purple rock everywhere.)

'Before you combust from excitement, could someone tell me if we are in the *correct* place?' said Nix impatiently.

'The Optimum Time is almost upon us.

We have precisely nineteen Earthling minutes and forty-seven Earthling seconds remaining. We do not have time for *celebrations.*'

(Ah.)

I had been **so excited** about returning to Earth that I had *almost forgotten* about our looming

END-OF-THE-WORLD-AS-WE-KNOW-IT

DEADLINE.

'We're in the right place,' I said. I pointed to the large building in front of us. 'That's Twiddle Manor.'

Nix peered through the screen. A short distance ahead of us, past a pair of open metal gates, was a vast manor house. A red carpet led towards the entrance, flanked by two lines of towering **rainbow-coloured** trees. In front of the entrance were dozens of stalls. An **ENORMOUS** banner with the words

HAPPY HALF-CENTURY DAY

floated above the manor roof, suspended in place by a pair of winged **ROBOTIC** birds.

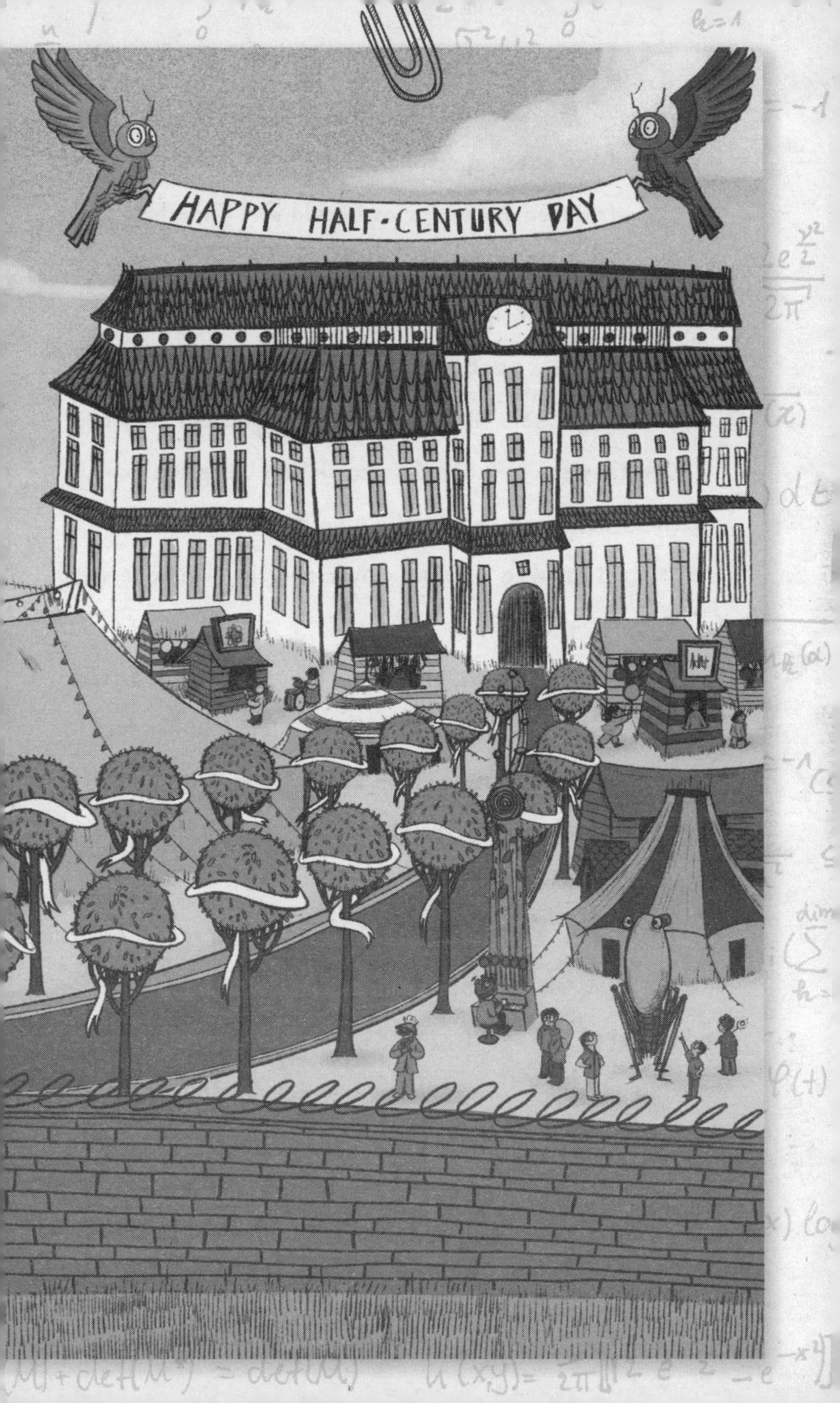
HAPPY HALF-CENTURY DAY

Beyond the gates, a number of custard-yellow marquees stretched out as far as I could see. The whole place was BURSTING with YOUNG INVENTORS. They moved between the marquees like ants, clutching various **peculiar devices**.

'Earthlings,' said Nix. 'How blissfully ignorant they are.'

'Can they see us?' asked Bean, sitting up on the bunk. He looked tired and a little pale, but his arm had returned to its usual colour and the skin no longer looked scaly.

'No, nada, **no**,' said Nix. 'The ship is fitted with camouflage shields.' She leapt to her feet.

'We now have seventeen Earthling minutes and fifty Earthling seconds until The Optimum Time. Where is the trophy of Zirboonium?'

'The **Brain Trophy** will be in the judging room,' I said. 'I don't know where that is, but we'll figure it out once we're there.'

Nix nodded. 'You have done enough, Earthlings. I will deal with Goospa myself.' Before I could understand what she *meant*, she'd whipped the door open and slipped out. It shut instantly behind her.

'Door seal activated,' said an automated voice above us.

'Uh – Nix?' I ran to the door and tried the handle. The door **WOULDN'T BUDGE.**

'What is she doing?' said Broccoli.

'Nix, you can't _LEAVE US HERE!_' I shouted, tugging the handle as hard as I could.

'This is between me and my brother,' echoed Nix's voice from the other side of the door. 'Fear not. I will make sure Goospa does not teleport your planet.'

'Nix! Open this door **RIGHT NOW!**' I tried the handle again.

'NIX!'

'I think she's gone,' said Bean.

I dashed past him to the console. 'I can't believe she's left us here! Who does she think she is? She doesn't stand a chance of stopping Goospa without our help.' I jabbed a few of the buttons, hoping one of them would unlock the door.

The console beeped rudely back at me.

'There has to be something here that will open it.'

'Come on,' muttered Broccoli, trying the handle again.

'It's no good, Broccoli,' I said. 'It's SEALED.' I **jiggled** an orange lever up and down.

The console beeped again.

EURGH.

'We're running out of time,' said Broccoli. 'We've only got sixteen minutes left.'

'You don't need to remind me,' I said impatiently, frantically **punching** and **pushing every button** and lever in sight.

'Can you give me a hand here?'

'Archibald?' said Bean behind us. 'Broccoli, I can't see Archie.'

'I'm a little busy right now,' said Broccoli, flicking buttons on the left-hand side of the console. 'Esha, haven't you got something in your Inventor's Kit we can use?'

I pretended not to hear him.

'Esha?' said Broccoli sternly. 'Where's your Inventor's Kit?'

'I don't have it!' I said. 'I fell into the crater and everything dropped out.'

'You lost your Inventor's Kit (again?) said Broccoli incredulously. 'I thought you'd put a button on that pocket!'

'Is this really *helpful* right now?' I snapped.

'Archibald?' said Bean.

Suddenly a button pinged off the top right of the console.

SHOT

I ducked as a lever into the air after it.

Blue and white sparks FIZZ-WHIZZED across the panel.

'What's going on?' cried Broccoli.

'I don't know - you must have done something!'

'Me? But—'

There was a loud hiss behind us.

'Look!' said Bean. 'The door - it's open!'

'It is? I mean, of course it is!' I grinned at Broccoli. 'Told you that pressing all those buttons would work. We must have—'

'Archibald!' said Bean.

I looked down.

Creeping out from behind the console, looking **EXTREMELY** pleased with himself, was Archibald. A coil of wires was **dangling** from his mouth.

'Archie?' said Broccoli. He lifted his **EVIL reptile** into the air and gently pulled the wires out of his mouth. 'Was that **you? Did you** open the door?'

Archibald rolled his eyes and made a noise that sounded like, 'Well, _someone_ had to step in.'

'Oh, you clever tortoise!' said Broccoli. 'Isn't he a clever tortoise, Esha?'

EURGH.

I cleared my throat. 'Well – I suppose – I mean we don't know for definite it was him—'

'You're a hero, Archie!' said Broccoli.

'He did all right,' I said reluctantly.

Archibald gave me a smug look.

'For a tortoise,' I added quickly.

'Now let's go – we have a

planet teleportation to S̲T̲O̲P̲!̲'

'I'm coming, too,' said Bean. He **wobbled** out of the bunk, his legs trembling a little as he stood up. He still looked pale, but his eyes were fierce and determined. 'I want to help.'

'Fine,' I said, already running towards the open door. 'Just make sure you keep up.'

How (Not) to
Save the World

We raced out of the KOOPLARZA, sprinting past
the rainbow-coloured trees up the red carpet towards the
manor.

'Which way do we go?' puffed Bean behind us.

'I don't know,' I panted, pausing at the first stall.
'We don't have the map.'

People streamed in and out of the manor, bustling
past us in excitement. From the direction of the marquees
came a series of whistles, **BANGS** and pops, alongside
a loud jingling of music. 'Welcome, one and all,' said
a voice over a loudspeaker. 'Welcome, one and all, to
GENIE's Half-Century Day! We hope
you are having a brain-bending day of
INVENTING BRILLIANCE. Please note that entries to the
Young Inventor of the Year contest are now closed, and all
inventions have been securely stored in the judging room.
The judging will commence shortly!'

'Look at that!' said a **rabbit-eared boy** beside us. He pointed behind my head. 'That looks like a **spaceship!**'

I turned around and realized he was pointing at the KOOPLARZA, which was definitely NOT invisible any more. People were already gathering around it, their faces bright with curiosity.

Oh well. We had **far** more important things to worry about than camouflage shields.

'Further announcements about the contest will follow soon,' continued the voice on the speaker. *'In the meantime, please continue to enjoy your day of inventing.'*

'This place is **ENORMOUS,**' said Broccoli. He checked his watch. 'We've got thirteen minutes until The Optimum Time. We **have** to find the judging room, now! And what about all these people? Shouldn't we get them out of here? We don't want anyone getting hurt.'

'You're right.' I looked around at the inventors. They had **NO IDEA** we were minutes away from an alien SHOWDOWN. 'But how do we get them to leave?'

'Remember to have your photograph taken in the Edison tent,' boomed the voice above us over the loudspeaker. 'And you can design a brand-new invention in one of the many Inventor Workshops—'

'I've got it!' cried Bean, pointing to the speaker. 'Leave it to me. I'll make sure everyone gets out.'

I stared at him, just a (teensy-tiny) bit impressed. Maybe Broccoli's cousin wasn't such a pustule, after all. 'I'll find the judging room,' I said.

Broccoli hesitated, glancing between the two of us.

'Go with Bean,' I said gently. 'We can't let him go on his own. Not while he's still recovering from that vilter sting.'

'What about you?' said Broccoli.

'I'll be fine,' I said, giving him what I hoped was a convincing smile. 'I'm Esha Verma. **Genius inventor** extraordinaire. There isn't anyone in or out of this galaxy that can defeat me. Besides, if we're lucky, Goospa might not have arrived yet – he's on a bike and we were on a spaceship, remember? If I can find the judging room in time, I can get to the **Brain Trophy** before him and Nix. Just keep an eye out for anyone that looks like me. It might *not* be . . . well . . . me.'

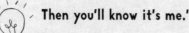

'How will we know if it's you or Goospa?' said Bean. 'You look identical.'

'Ask for a code word,' I said. 'Lightbulb. Then you'll know it's me.'

'But what if he *is* in the judging room?' asked Broccoli, his snot wobbling anxiously. 'How will you **stop** him?'

'I'll think of something,' I said, already moving off into the crowd.

'ESHA!' shouted Broccoli after me. '**YOU DON'T HAVE A PLAN,** DO YOU?'

I could still hear him calling my name as I disappeared into the throng of inventors. There must have been *hundreds* of them. The air crackled and sparkled with their SPINGLY-TINGLY excitement as I sped past them to the manor entrance.

'Get your latest edition of the *Inventor's Handbook* here!'

shouted a purple-haired woman behind a stall.

'The ultimate Inventor's Toolbox! Custom-made for all your gadgets and gizmos!'

I sprinted past them through the doors, wishing, more than anything, that I had a moment to stop and look around the stalls. After all, this was GENIE's

ONCE-IN-A-LIFETIME
HALF-CENTURY DAY.

I should have been here, unveiling my Inviz-Whiz and WINNING the **Brain Trophy** in style. Instead, I was trying to **stop** an alien who wanted to **steal** Earth for blueberries.

 EURGH.

Sometimes, life was just

NOT FAIR.

Through the doors was a large, bustling hallway covered with the same red carpet. There was a large clock fixed to the wall opposite the entrance. Above the clock was a banner with curly writing, which said:

GENIUS WAITS FOR NO ONE.

I stopped and glanced around the hall: there was a doorway to the left, another to the right, and more stairs leading up to another floor. Unfortunately, there wasn't a single sign that told me where I could find the judging room.

I glanced at the clock again: 3.20 p.m. There was only ten minutes left until The Optimum Time.

Then I saw a pair of girls huddled over a map in the corner. 'Hello – excuse me,' I said, darting over. 'Can I borrow that?'

Before they could answer, I *snatched* the map from them and scanned it for the judging room. There it was! Through the doors on the left and down the corridor.

'Hey!' said one of the girls as I sped off, still clutching the map. 'That's mine—'

I dived through the doors and into a NARROW corridor, my trainers squeaking across the floor as I ran. At the end of the corridor I found it –
a door with a sign marked →

THE JUDGING ROOM.

My stomach did a little flip.

This was IT.

Behind this door was **THE Brain Trophy**.

I glanced either side of me.

There was no sign of Goospa.

Maybe I had beaten him to it.

I put my hand on the door handle.

To my complete surprise, the door slid open.

I frowned.

I had expected the judging room to be locked, so this was either a stroke of VERY good luck or . . . I glanced at the door again, suddenly noticing something that I hadn't seen before.

The lock was broken.

I took a deep breath. Then I took another step forward and opened the door, just a crack. I peeped through.

A short distance away from me, in the centre of an
ENORMOUS room, was . . . <u>ME.</u>

In the *same* dungarees.

With the *same* ponytail and the *same*
inventioning hairband.

GOOSPA.

On either side of the room there were two long
tables with all the entries for the **Brain Trophy** laid
out. Beneath each entry was a piece of parchment with
its name and function. I could just about make out the few
closest to me:

The ULTIMATE
PICNIC-PROTECTOR BLANKET –
Never have your picnic disturbed
by a wasp, bee or fly again!

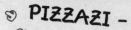

PIZZAZI –
Slice a pizza
in milliseconds!

FLOWER FINDER –
The ultimate flower identifier,
for home and abroad.

At the front of the room, held inside a clear glass case, was the trophy itself, the brain-shaped Zirboonium sparkling a beautiful, brilliant green.

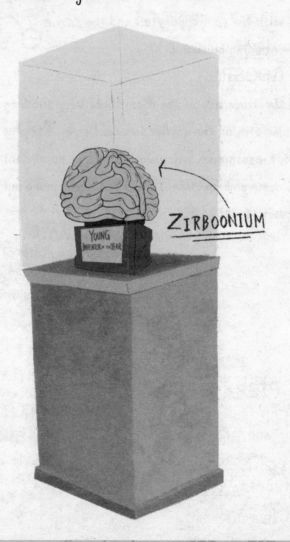

ZIRBOONIUM

YOUNG
INVENTOR OF THE YEAR

I hesitated. Part of me knew I should go back and find Broccoli and Bean. But we had less than ten minutes until The Optimum Time. If I was going to stop Goospa, I had to do it now.

And I had a plan.

Well, half of one.

Or a quarter.

OK, so maybe it wasn't really a plan yet. More of an idea-in-progress.

I checked my pockets and pulled out the only item that I had left: a yo-yo.

You, the Reader, may be thinking that this was no ordinary yo-yo. You may be thinking that it was a special invention in the form of a yo-yo, an invention that could easily stop an alien. Well, you would be **WRONG.**

This yo-yo was, in fact, only a yo-yo. But Goospa didn't know that.

I slid the yo-yo back into my pocket, took another deep breath, then flung open the door.

'Goospa, stop!' I shouted.

He turned around, his eyes widening.

'Esha-Verma-Verma-Esha.' He blinked slowly. I stepped back. It was so ODD to see your reflection standing in front of you. 'I did not expect to see you. Har-Har-Har.'

'It's over, Goospa,' I said. 'Move away from the trophy.'

'But you are too late. Har-Har-Har.' He held up a **large** ball, which seemed to be composed of a peculiar combination of wires, twine, something that might have been a metal trowel, and –

'Are those *dinosaur droppings?*' I said incredulously.

'A necessary inclusion, Earthling. The device is almost ready. All I require is the Zirboonium.'

'If you teleport Earth, you could (destroy) the *entire galaxy,*' I said, repeating what Nix had told us. 'You can't just move a planet from one dimension to another. Not without accounting for *all* the variables. If you get it wrong, you could—'

'Har-Har-Har. Do not teach me about dimensional physics, puny Earthling,' said Goospa. 'At The Optimum Time, Earth will be transported to the Newporla Dimension. There is nothing you can do.'

'That's what *you* think.' I whipped out the yo-yo and held it in front of me. 'See this?' I said. 'This is a . . . **SPATIAL HOOVER DEVICE.** My newest and **deadliest** invention. Move any closer to that trophy and I will **activate** it.'

Goospa blinked again. Then –

'Har-Har-Har,' he shrieked, his whole body shaking with laughter. 'Har-Har-Har. Har-Har. Do you really think you can **fool** me, Earthling? Spatial hoover device! Har-Har-Har. That is an **Earthling toy.**'

I flushed.

OK, so maybe Goospa *did* know about yo-yos.

Before I could think of a suitable genius response, footsteps thudded into the room behind me.

'Did you find . . .' began Broccoli, trailing off as he caught sight of Goospa. He looked between the two of us, his eyes **widening**. 'Oh.'

'Broccoli, what are you doing here?' I hissed. 'You're supposed to be with Bean—' I stopped as I caught sight of his feet. On one foot was his shoe; on the other was a green wellington. 'What are you wearing?'

'Borrowed it from a stall. Lost my other shoe, remember? Archibald's looking after Bean – I thought you might need my help.'

At that moment, a curly-haired man, with a cap labelled SECURITY, appeared in the doorway.

'What do you kids think you're doing in here? This room should be locked. How did you—' His eyes widened in surprise as he caught sight of me, then Goospa-me. He scratched the top of his cap. 'Twins, eh? Well, fancy that. Now go on. Get out of here, all of you. The judges will be arriving soon.'

'I am not going anywhere, puny Earthling,' said Goospa.

'Puny Earthling?' said the guard. He frowned and pointed to his badge. 'My name is Terence. Terence Baggs.'

'I am not going anywhere, puny Terence Baggs,'

said Goospa. He began to glide towards the case containing the **Brain Trophy**. 'I have **important** business here.'

'Er – don't go near that, please,' said Terence.

'**What shall we do, Broccoli?**' I whispered desperately. But my apprentice didn't appear to be listening. Instead, he was peering at the inventions on the table beside him.

[A note from Broccoli: I was, in fact, trying to make a plan because we did not have one.]

'Excuse me? Did you hear what I said?' Terence pushed past us and stepped in front of Goospa, his hands on his hips. 'Please leave the room,' he said, a new firmness in his voice. '**Now.**'

'Out of my way, Terence Baggs,' said Goospa.

Just then, the loudspeaker rang out.

'*This is an emergency announcement,*' declared a (familiar) voice, booming across the room. '*A very official emergency announcement.*'

Bean! I smiled. That **annoying pimple** had actually **done it.**

'There is an – uh – *emergency.*' Bean's voice echoed out of the tannoy across the room. '*One of the inventions has* malfunctioned. *All visitors to the GENIE contest are asked to leave by the nearest exit as quickly as—*'

'What in the—' Terence said, looking **baffled**.

'*Did you all* **HEAR** *that?*' continued the announcement. '*You must get out of here* right NOW!

Get out!

'Esha,' whispered Broccoli. He motioned to one of the inventions that looked like a bright yellow cauldron with a small cannon poking out of it. 'Look at this.'

'This isn't the time to admire inventions, Broccoli,' I replied fiercely. I was gauging the distance between me and the **Brain Trophy**, assessing whether I could reach it before Goospa, who was still trying to get past Terence.

Answer: Unlikely but *not impossible*.

Not impossible seemed like our best option right now. Trying not to make any noise, I slipped behind the table on the other side of the room and began to edge along the wall towards the trophy.

'This is your last chance, Terence Baggs,' hissed Goospa. 'I shall not ask again. Move out of my way.'

'I'm afraid not,' said Terence. 'You heard the announcement. An invention has *malfunctioned* and we need to evacuate. I will escort you kids to the nearest exit. Follow me, please.'

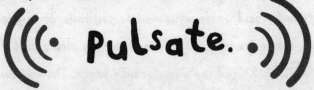

'I shall not,' said Goospa.

Terence scratched his cap again. Clearly, he hadn't been trained to deal with this kind of situation. 'Right, well then.' He moved a hand towards the walkie-talkie clipped to his belt. 'In that case, I'll just have to call . . .'

His voice trailed off.

Goospa had started to shake. No, not shake –

$$(((\bullet \; \mathsf{Pulsate.} \; \bullet)))$$

A flash of yellow light shone around his body. I stepped back against the wall, shielding my eyes from the brightness.

A series of horrible **POP-CRUNCH-POP** noises
echoed through the air. Moments later, he was

TOWERING

ABOVE US

in his true form, his orange robes swishing around him.
(UH OH.)

Whimpering, Terence took a step back.

I edged closer. I was almost level with Goospa now, the
Brain Trophy gleaming a short distance ahead of me.

Out of the corner of my eye, I saw Broccoli slip behind
the other table and position himself behind the invention
he had shown me earlier.

What on earth was he doing?

'Enough,' said Goospa. His arm darted towards Terence's
walkie-talkie. He whipped it into his mouth with a loud
CRUNCH. 'Out of my way, Terence Baggs. The Optimum
Time is almost upon us, Har-Har. I must ready the
TELEPORTATION DEVICE.'

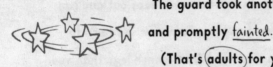

The guard took another step back —

and promptly <u>fainted</u>.

(That's (adults) for you.)

That's when Goospa noticed me, lurking behind the table.

We stared at each other for a moment, eyelids quivering

in the **ULTIMATE**

NO-BLINKING

contest.

'Are you listening?' said Bean's

voice over the tannoy.

Exit for
emergency
use only

'This is an **emergency**, people!

EVACUATE!'

Without a second's hesitation, I leapt out and ran towards the **Brain Trophy**. Turns out it's hard to outsprint an alien who has MUCH longer legs than you. Before I could get close, Goospa was already in front of the glass case, the trophy glittering inside it.

'Goospa, stop!' shouted Broccoli from behind the other table. 'You don't know what you're doing! You could destroy the *whole galaxy*.'

Goospa ignored him, lifted up the case and pulled out the **Brain Trophy** –

A moment later, a **GIANT** glittery

CUSTARD PIE

whizzed across the air

and landed

on top of his head

with a loud **SQUELCH.**

➡ What in the . . . ?

Goospa turned around, **startled.** Another

 custard pie smacked

against his arm. I turned to

see Broccoli standing over

the cauldron-like invention, his face bright with

determination.

'I *told you* to **STOP!**' he shouted.

'That is most impolite, Earthling,' growled Goospa.

Seizing this GOLDEN opportunity, I sped forward

and snatched the trophy out of his

hands, as a third custard pie splattered

against his shoulder.

'Broccoli, what is that?' I yelled

as I sprinted back towards him. 'It's

BRILLIANT!'

'The **Glitter Custard Cannon,**' he shouted, aiming

the cylinder at Goospa. 'Designed by Augustus Trott. Eight

years old. Thank you, Augustus!'

'Give me the Zirboonium, Earthling,' rumbled Goospa,

the floor shaking a little as he lumbered after me.

'I'll cover you!' cried Broccoli as another custard pie

zoomed over my head. 'Get the Zirboonium out of here!'

'Enough,' snarled Goospa, batting the pie away.

'ESHA, WATCH OUT!' shouted Broccoli.

I glanced back just in time to see Goospa seize a **banana-shaped invention** from the table and hurl it towards me. I dived sideways and rolled across the floor, the contraption landing on the carpet an arm's length away from me.

'EVACUATE!' boomed Bean's voice. *'This is an* **emergency!'**

'The trophy is mine, Esha-Verma-Verma-Esha,' growled Goospa. He was only a short distance behind me now.

SPLAT! SPLAT! More custard pies kerzoomed over my head, missing me, but hitting my **slimy** opponent.

'PREPOSTERATIONS!' howled Goospa.

'MOVE, ESHA!' yelled Broccoli. 'WE'VE ONLY GOT A FEW MINUTES UNTIL THE OPTIMUM TIME!'

If I could keep the Zirboonium away from Goospa until The Optimum Time had passed, we were safe. Holding on to the **Brain Trophy**, I leapt to my feet and sprinted towards the doorway.

SPLAT! SPLAT! SPLAT!

As I ran, dodging other inventions being hurled in my direction, a shrill whining sound screeched across the speaker. This was followed by a loud BLOP! noise, which sounded suspiciously like a modified marshmallow. BLOP! BLOP!

'HA! Take that! And that! I might have lost my slingshot, but I can still throw! Isn't that right, Archie? Isn't that—'

There was the sound of a scuffle, then –

'Hello,' said a different, harassed-sounding voice on the speaker. 'Please **ignore** the previous announcement. No one evacuate. None of the inventions have malfunctioned. There was a security breach, but everything is *fine* now. I repeat, everything is fine. **No one evacuate—**'

Behind me, the custard cannon made a **rude noise**; a trail of smoke puffed out of the top.

'I think it might be **overheating!**'
said Broccoli, stepping back.

Honestly. Some inventors just
don't have what it takes.

Still, I was *nearly* at the door.
I ran, heart pounding. Eight steps – seven –

There was another loud whine over the speaker then –

 'Give that back!' said the same harassed
voice. 'Someone get him out of—
Is that a tortoise? **AAAGH** – it bites!'

There was an ear-splitting whine, then the speaker cut
out completely.

Four steps from the doorway –

'TAKE COVER!' shouted Broccoli, throwing himself to the
floor. *'Malfunction!'*

BOOM!

I ducked as the machine exploded, **custard blobs** and
glitter whizzing across the room, then staggered on.

Three steps – two –

THWACK!

Something caught the back of my foot, sending me

c a r t w h e e l i n g

through the air. The **Brain Trophy** whizzed out of my hand.

'CATCH IT!' I shouted as I tumbled to the ground.

Broccoli sprinted towards it. **'I've got it!** I've—'

With a flick of his arm, Goospa whipped the trophy out of mid-air towards himself. 'Enough of your games, puny Earthlings,' he said. 'The Optimum Time is now upon us.'

With *terrifying* speed, he snapped the Zirboonium off the trophy and slid it inside his teleportation device, which started to hum loudly. Before Broccoli or I could move, he flicked a button on the bottom of the contraption. It shot into the air, filling the room with a sea-green light.

OH NO.

That's when the door was flung open.

The Anomalizer

Nix stood in the doorway. She blinked in bewilderment as she spotted me and Broccoli.

'How did you two . . .' Her voice trailed off as she saw Goospa, the teleporter hovering in the air above him. A *scowl* twisted across her face. Without another word, she strode forward. 'At last. **I found you, Goospa.**'

Goospa looked bewildered. 'Who are you and how do you know my name?'

Nix **glared** at him.

He stared at her for a moment, his eyes **widening**.

'Nix? Har-Har. You changed your appearance too. Har-Har.' He backed away, sounding less sure of himself now. 'How did you get here? Har-Har. How did you find me?'

'You hijacked my ship and made us crash on a No-Go planet,' spat Nix, folding her arms. 'My KOOPLARZA landed in a VILTER CRATER.'

'A vilter crater?' said Goospa. 'Har-Har. A pity I missed it.'

'You think it is amusing?' said Nix. 'I have faced  and a LAVA MARSH. I lost my planet buggy. I have been forced to come to this silly planet and I was detained at a ludicrous Inventor Workshop. Candyfloss Crafts. And you find it *amusing?*' Her voice shook with fury. 'Stop that device now. I will not let you teleport Earth for The Pa and The Ma's Grand Re-Crowning. You are coming with me to PADRRU.'

'You are **TOO LATE,** dear sister.' Goospa glanced up at his device with an arrogant smirk. 'The teleportation process has been initiated. I may be the youngest, but now the others will bow to me. Including <u>you.</u>'

'Bow to you?' said Nix. 'You do not know the first thing about teleportation or DIMENSIONAL PHYSICS.'

She pointed to the teleporter. 'That is going to destroy the *ENTIRE GALAXY* if we do not STOP it – including our planet, Zelpha. Do you think The Ma and The Pa will be pleased with *that?*'

'Har-Har,' said Goospa. 'You cannot fool me. I know *exactly* what I am doing. The Pa and The Ma will have an endless supply of the Earthly **blue-berry** thanks to **me**.'

Shielding my face from the green light, I saw that the teleporter had started to *spin*. A shrill whistling noise rang through the air. Broccoli clapped his hands over his ears.

'Prepare yourself, Earthlings,' said Goospa. 'Har-Har. Soon, Earth will be teleported to the Newporla Dimension.' He glowered at Nix. 'And you will no longer be the favourite of The Pa and The Ma or the Crown Princess. Instead, they will make **me** the Crown Prince.'

'Favourite?' echoed Nix. 'You think I **want** to be the favourite? Where do you think I was taking the **KOOPLARZA** before you snuck on board and ruined everything? I was *running away*, Goospa, to join PADRRU. NOW WILL YOU  *STOP*

 *THAT DEVICE!'*

The whistling noise grew even more SHRILL.

'Running away?' said Goospa. He hesitated. A confused expression crossed his slimy face. 'Why would you run away? You are the favourite of The Pa and The Ma. You are the Crown Princess.'

'Because the Crown Princess of Zelpha does not join

PADRRU,' said Nix bitterly. 'The Pa and The Ma do not care that I have been selected. So I ran away. In fact, I would be at PADRRU HQ at this very moment if you had not tried to steal my ship!'

'This is all *very* interesting, but we don't have time for a family reunion!' I cried, standing between them. 'Tell us how to stop that thing!'

Just then, the teleporter whizzed higher into the air, gave a short, piercing whistle, then . . .

BOOM!

The green light pulsed over us, shooting out across the room, through the windows, wrapping the sky in that same sea-green glow.

Footsteps echoed in the corridor, followed by a **BURST** of frantic voices.

'What's going on!'

'Look outside!'

I glanced towards the windows.

'Oh no,' whispered Broccoli.

Something **STRANGE** was happening to the sky. Enormous spirals of red were breaking through the clouds, which swirled and twisted as if they were caught inside an enormous mixer.

Streaks of black lightning flashed across it. A moment later, the Earth **SHOOK** like there was a herd of rhinos about to **stampede** their way into the judging room. Some of the inventions slid off the tables and crashed to the floor.

'I did not know,' said Goospa quietly. He was staring at Nix with a perplexed look on his face, completely oblivious to everything else happening around us. 'You did not say.'

'You did **not ask!**' retorted Nix. 'If you had told me you wanted to be the Crown Prince, I would have gladly accompanied you to speak to The Pa and The Ma. Instead, you devised this ridiculous plan and now you have put the entire galaxy in danger!'

'What's happening here?' said a voice behind us.

I whirled around.

My eyes **widened**.

There, in the doorway, were none other than the

GENIE judges.

(As if things weren't bad enough already.)
_____

They were dressed in a colourful assortment of lab coats — red, green, yellow, each labelled with the word JUDGE. Each coat was fitted with a glorious assortment of pockets of different shapes and sizes.

'This is — unexpected,' said the judge at the front. He had a thick cloud of curly black hair, which bounced lightly from one side to the other as he looked between us. He was wearing a bubblegum-pink lab coat and

fluffy yellow trainers. A pair of star-shaped sunglasses was tucked into one pocket. On another pocket, stitched in lilac letters, were the words:

HEAD JUDGE.

Oh dear.

'Uh — well . . .' I glanced at Broccoli, who shrugged unhelpfully. 'I can absolutely explain. You see—'

'Marvellous inventing outfit,' said another judge, catching sight of Goospa.

A spiral of light flashed out of the teleporter and shot across the room towards the judges. They dived sideways, the head judge throwing himself left whilst the others leapt towards the right.

Plaster and paint fell off the ceiling as the teleporter moved higher, zapping bolts of light.

CRACK!

A colossal zigzag suddenly *splintered* across the floor, splitting it in two, with us on one side and the judges on the other.

Goospa took a step back. He looked frightened and rather small. 'I do not understand. Har-Har. What is all this?'

'What I was trying to tell you, Goospa!' bellowed Nix. 'You cannot teleport one planet to another dimension without endangering the inter-planetary forces.'

'But this was The Optimum Time,' said Goospa. 'I checked the THEORETICAL THEOREM. It said nothing of this!'

'Exactly how much of the theorem did you read?' shouted Nix.

'Well – I—'

'There are countless variables that must be considered

for planetary teleportation. That is why it is considered
too dangerous!'

CRACK!

Another zigzag ripped through the floor.

Goospa whimpered and backed away towards the wall.

'Goospa!' thundered Nix as **more**
inventions crashed to the floor. 'If we
do not stop this now, this *entire planet* will
be **destroyed** and the galaxy along with it!'

'I – I can't,' said Goospa. He ducked as a whirl of
electric light danced out of the device like an *eel*, almost
singeing his antenna. 'I do not know how!'

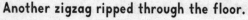

'Didn't you fix it with a fail-safe?' I asked.

'What is that?' said Goospa.

I g°ggled at him.

'You *must* have some kind of **STOP**
function!' shouted Broccoli.

STOP

'I did not think of that,' said Goospa, his voice barely
audible over the noise of the device. He was quivering
unhelpfully in the corner of the room. 'This is terrible,
Har-Har. This is most terrible!'

Another bolt of light crackled through the air.

Nix dived under a table, motioning us to follow.

'It is not too late!' she said, huddling beside us.

We can still stop the teleporter – if we can just find

a way to disrupt its **SPATIAL ENERGY!'**

'How do we do that?' I yelled.

'We can't even get near it!' added Broccoli.

Inventions CRASHED to the floor

as more light crackled across the room.

'Spatial mechanics!' said Nix. 'Multiple spatial energies

cannot co-exist – there would be too much interference –

they would **destroy** each other. We need something

that generates the same amount of spatial energy as the

teleporter. Then they will cancel each other out.'

'Why?' I said.

'Now is not the time to explain,

Earthling!' she said. 'What we need is

another device that can generate its own

spatial energy!'

'But we don't have anything!' said Broccoli. 'So what do

we do?'

'I – well—' blustered Nix, staring at the teleporter in fright. 'We – we need to . . . I am not sure.'

I glanced between the alien siblings; they both looked **lost** and *scared*. A *horrible* cold sensation flooded over me as the teleporter spun faster and faster. If Nix and Goospa didn't know what to do, then WE WERE DOOMED.

We had no Inventor's Kit.

No SPINGLY-TINGLY ideas.

To make everything worse, it was ALL *my fault*. If it hadn't been for the Inviz-Whiz, then none of this would have . . .

Wait a moment.

I looked at the teleportation device, a single ZINGING lightbulb moment illuminating my brain cells. It was **ridiculous**, improbable, but maybe, just maybe –

'What if we create a spatial anomaly?' I shouted.

'An anomaly?' echoed Broccoli. 'You mean a **portal?**' He was clinging to the table leg, his snot bouncing quicker than a **kangaroo** in a boxing match. 'How will that help?'

'Remember what happened with the Inviz-Whiz?

We opened a portal to another planet — the Inviz-Whiz had to generate *spatial energy* to do that!' I looked at Nix. 'You just said that *multiple spatial energies can't be in the same place at the same time or they'll destroy each other*. So what if we build another Inviz-Whiz to destroy Goospa's teleporter? Could that work?'

She hesitated.

'Yes or no, Nix?' I bellowed.

'I suppose — yes — theoretically! But how will we build one? We have **NO** tools, **NO** instruments!'

Another bolt of light crackled over us.

'We can use what's here!' cried Broccoli, his face lighting up. He waved a hand at the *broken inventions* scattered around us. 'Work with what we have! That's what **true inventing** is all about!'

'Exactly!' I said, my chest puffing up with **ULTIMATE** pride for my apprentice. 'Chapter 1 of the *Inventor's Handbook: You will only be a true inventor when you invent something out of not very much at all*.'

(I had taught him well.)

I slid out from under the table, dashed over to the nearest pile of **inventions** and began **rummaging** through them.

'We'll need string – lots of it! And wires – a conductor—'

'It will need to be powerful,' said Nix. She glanced fearfully at Goospa's device, which was *crackling* and *spinning* even faster. 'If it does not generate enough **SPATIAL ENERGY,** it may not be strong enough to disrupt the teleporter.'

'Then we have to make it **bigger** than the Inviz-Whiz!' shouted Broccoli. **'A lot bigger!'**

'What do you think you're doing?' **thundered** a voice. Glancing over my shoulder, I saw the head judge glaring at me from the corner of the room.

'DO NOT TOUCH those inventions! That is

SABOTAGE!'

'Sorry, Mr Head Judge, sir,' I cried.
'But I don't have a choice!'

'What do you—'

Ignoring the judge, I ripped a long metal coil out of the invention in front of me. Nix and Broccoli flitted around the room, dodging lightning bolts and ripping the inventions to pieces, as I fired instructions at them.

Pushing all **end-of-the-world** thoughts out of my mind, I worked at triple-quick speed, threading and stitching pieces of various inventions together into a single, sensational device:

THE ANOMALIZER.

I (wish) I could tell you exactly what we used to make the Anomalizer, but NASA have warned me that they will **REDACT** this information if I try. So I cannot tell you that we used ▮▮▮▮▮ and ▮▮▮▮▮ and ▮▮▮▮▮ .

(What did I tell you? Apparently, NASA are afraid it might encourage others to build Anomalizers, which could be *extremely dangerous.* Ridiculous, I know.)

'What else do we need?' shouted Nix.

'A conductor!' I said. 'Something small. About the size of—No, wait! I've got it!' I ripped the button from the pocket on my dungarees and tied it across the device with a shoelace. **'Done!'**

At that moment, an **ENORMOUS** bolt of light snapped towards me.

Why I, Esha Verma, Am a <u>Genius</u>

'ESHA, **WATCH OUT!**' yelled Broccoli.

I leapt out of the way, the Anomalizer whizzing out of my hand.

'**NO!**' I cried as it **bounced** across the floor – once, twice, three times – and teetered over the crack in the floor. Scrambling to my feet, I leapt towards it, fingers outstretched . . . but the Anomalizer went over the edge. I threw myself forward, the top half of my body **dangling dangerously** over the precipice as I grabbed the Velcro handle in my left hand.

'GOT IT!' I shouted.

Only I had leaned out a **little further** than I should have.

OK, maybe a lot further.

I felt myself slipping downwards with the weight of the Anomalizer, the dark chasm of the Earth staring at me from below.

'*HELP!*' I yelled, trying (and failing) to wriggle back.

Everyone was shouting above me.

'ESHA!'

'GET OUT OF THERE!'

'*HELP ME!*' I yelled.

'ESHA!'

For a second, I was quite certain that one voice belonged to Nishi, but it was impossible to hear anything properly in all the (((**NOISE.**)))

'*HELP!*'

A moment later, I felt something take hold of my dungarees.

'I have you, Earthling,' grunted Goospa.

The Anomalizer swayed in the air, my arms shaking with its weight as he dragged me back to the surface. I rolled onto my back, clasping the Anomalizer tightly to my chest.

'It's – ready,' I panted.

'Will it work?' said Goospa, his eyes wide and frightened.

'Only one way to find out.'

CRACK!

Another zigzag ripped through the floor as the teleporter twisted faster and faster, the whole room glittering with its light.

'DO IT NOW!' shouted Nix and Broccoli together.

Murmuring a quick prayer to the inventing gods, I pressed the switch on the Anomalizer. Almost at once, it started to rattle, the whole contraption shaking back and forth. A second later, it leapt out of my hands onto the floor.

'What is it doing?' said Goospa.

Before I could reply, another bolt of light zapped down towards us. I leapt out of the way and crawled backwards towards the wall, Goospa close behind me.

We watched, eyes wide, as the Anomalizer rose into the air until it was level with Goospa's teleporter. The devices hovered alongside each other, bolts of electrical energy whizzing over our heads.

'Is it working?' cried Broccoli, poking his head out from under a table.

The Anomalizer was twisting back and forth, shaking and shimmying, fighting against the energy from the teleporter.

'Look!' said Nix. 'Can you see that?'

I NARROWED my eyes, following to where she was pointing.

That's when I saw it.

A **portal**, exactly like the one created by the Inviz-Whiz, was opening around the Anomalizer. At least, it was *trying* to open. The air appeared to be pulling a p a r t, exactly as it had done before. Only, as I watched, a zap from the teleporter closed the hole again. A bolt of electrical light shot out of the Anomalizer into the teleporter, which **trembled** violently. The electrical storm between the two battling inventions rose higher and higher, illuminating the room in wild corkscrews of greens, yellows, blues and whites.

'Take cover!' I ducked under the other table, Goospa squeezing in beside me.

'What if it doesn't work?' he said, pressing himself against the wall. 'The Ma and The Pa will be furious. They shall exile me from . . .' He whimpered. 'If this does not work, there will not be a Zelpha!'

Suddenly a piercing whistling sound ripped around the room. More cracks splintered through the ground. Both the teleporter and the Anomalizer shook wildly, then . . .

BOOM!

A wave of energy pulsed through the air, throwing the table – and us – across the room.

'OOF!' I groaned as I crash-landed painfully on the carpet. I opened my eyes s-l-o-w-l-y.

Balls of green and yellow light hovered above my head, crackling with the same energy as before.

OH NO.

Our plan had failed.

If history still existed after today, then I, Esha Verma, would be remembered not as a **genius inventor extraordinaire** – but as an inventor who had

destroyed the ENTIRE galaxy.

But then the whirlpool of lights above me flickered. Again and again, each time growing fainter and fainter, until they disappeared altogether. A soft breeze floated through the air, making me shiver.

My legs quivered under me as I stood up. Broccoli was sitting up on the other side of the room. He looked AWFUL. His hair was more tangled than a bird's nest caught in a storm, his jumper was covered in snot patches, there was a large tear in the knee of his jeans, and yet, for some reason, he was SMILING.

'Esha, look!' he said, pointing to a window.

'The sky! Look at the sky!'

I turned.

Past the window, the sky was – well – the sky. An ordinary sky. Clear blue with a few clouds. There was no sign of the red spirals, the lightning, or any other evidence of alien teleportation.

Goospa sat up with a groan. A moment later, Nix leapt up and darted to the teleporter, which had fallen in the centre of the room. Fragments of Zirboonium were scattered all around us, each one still gleaming a soft green colour.

'Super stars!' Nix skipped around the remains of the device in delight.

'WE DID IT!
SUPER SHIMMERING STARS!'

She circled round and pulled Goospa into a hug. 'We did it, Goos! We did it!'

He blinked in surprise. 'Yes, we did. Har-Har.'

Broccoli grinned.

I shook my head. (Family.) Same in **all** galaxies.

'As I said,' came a voice from behind us. I turned around as the **GENIE** head judge rose unsteadily on the other side of the room. 'This is unexpected.'

The Brain Trophy,
AKA Where It All Began

OH.

I had been so delighted about the Earth **NOT** being teleported that I had **almost-sort-of forgotten** about the competition. The head judge brushed off his lab coat. The other judges teetered to their feet behind him, **coughing** and **spluttering**, their faces streaked with dust. A large crowd had gathered behind them – inventors, the purple-haired lady from the stall, the girls I'd stolen the map from. They were all *staring* in silence.

I glanced around.

The ceiling had bits of plaster and paint hanging off it.

The windows were *smashed.*

There were scorch marks all over the walls.

All the contestants' inventions were totally and utterly in **RUINS.**

I *swallowed.*

Talk about an

absolute ↑ DISASTER.

'Well,' said the head judge. He picked his way over the floor, dancing over the cracks like a cat, until he was standing opposite me. There were still streaks of dust in his hair, and his pink lab coat was now covered with several grimy patches. He looked sternly at each of us in turn, his eyes finally settling on me. They were bright and beady and reminded me of an owl. 'Who is responsible for this?'

I cleared my throat and forced a smile onto my face.

'Hello, Head Judge – sir. My name is Esha Verma. **Genius inventor** extraordinaire. I am sure you have heard of me. *Pleasure* to meet you.'

He raised an eyebrow. 'I asked a question,' he said quietly. 'Who is responsible for this?'

'I – well . . .' I began, my brain *whirring* through all the ready-made excuses from the *Inventor's Handbook* – but it is difficult to think of an excuse when you are standing in front of the HEAD JUDGE of the BEST CONTEST in the ENTIRE world.

There was a low groan behind us. A moment later, the guard who had fainted earlier sat up.

'Terence Baggs,' said Goospa, who was standing beside him. 'Hello.'

The guard's eyes widened, his mouth opened and shut, then he *fainted* again.

I smiled awkwardly at the head judge. 'I think he might need *a cup of tea.*'

'ESHA!'

Before the judge could respond, a wellington-wearing *whirlwind* whizzed out of the audience.

'Nishi?' I said, as my sister looped around the crack towards me. 'I thought I heard your voice!'

'ESHA! YOU'RE OK!'

She threw herself at me with such **FORCE** that I felt all the breath go out of me.

'That's my daughter, let me through!' cried a voice. Pulling away from Nishi, I spotted Mum charging towards me. Her face was flushed, her hair, which was tied into a loose bun, was falling out of place, and – to my complete

and utter **SHOCK** – she did not have a phone attached to her ear. Instead, she was holding Berty, who **ROARED** in delight as he caught sight of me.

With another **ROAR,** he leapt out of her arms and **bounded** in my direction, his tail **waggling** in delight. I giggled as he jumped on top of me, his huge slobbery tongue licking my face.

'I think he missed you,' said Nishi, smiling.

'Esha!' puffed Mum, running up after him.

'Uh – hello, Mum,' I said, smiling awkwardly. 'I didn't expect to see you—'

She pulled me into a hug and kissed the top of my head. 'Thank goodness you're OK,' she said. 'I was **SO worried!'**

351

'Excuse me,' said the head judge. 'But I will ask this one more time. Who is <u>responsible</u> for this?'

I took a deep breath, avoiding Mum's eye.
'I suppose that's – well – it's probably *me*.
I'm **sorry** about breaking the inventions, but I didn't really have a choice. It was the only way to **stop—**'
'BROCCOLI!'

Bean shot across the room, a familiar green **blob** held in his hand. He high-fived Broccoli and beamed at us, his face shining.

'We did it! We saved the Earth!

And we got everyone to **evacuate**, didn't we, Archie? Well – most people.' He *glared* at the crowd. 'The ones who listened.'

Broccoli smiled and ruffled the top of his hair. 'You did great, Bean. Both you and Archie.'

Archibald made a noise that sounded like, 'It was mostly me, but he did well for human standards.'

'What did you guys *do* here?' said Bean, looking around. 'This place is an *EPIC mess.*'

The head judge folded his arms and looked at me. The sleeves of his lab coat looked slightly charred in places. 'I'm still waiting for an explanation. For the final time: What happened here?'

'What happened is that we just saved this planet,' said Bean before I could reply. He stuck his hand out towards the head judge. 'Oliver Betty Darwin, otherwise known as Bean. You may call me the SAVIOUR of EARTH.'

(Clearly he had recovered from the vilter sting.)

'Saviour?' said the head judge.

'Yup. If it wasn't for us, this planet would have been TELEPORTED to a whole other dimension.'

'Bean,' I hissed, nudging him in the ribs.

(Honestly, he really didn't know when to stop talking.)

The judge raised his eyebrows. 'True genius must always believe in the unbelievable, but this . . . this sounds most far-fetched.'

I knew I should speak up, try and convince him, but I wasn't sure **what** to say or **where** to start.

'I – well . . .' I began.

I could feel Mum waiting expectantly beside me. Glancing over my shoulder, I looked at Nix and Goospa, who had been watching in silence.

Nix whispered something to Goospa, who nodded. A moment later, Nix began to

SHAKE.

A wave of shocked murmurs rippled across the room as she **TRANSFORMED**, shapeshifting into the same form as Goospa.

'That's **no inventing outfit!**' shouted a voice opposite the room.

Bean **giggled**. 'No way.'

Mum grabbed hold of me and Nishi, pulling us behind her.

'Is that – *IS THAT*—'

'It's an alien, Mum,' I said. I slid out of her grasp and stepped in front of her. 'But you don't have to be **scared**. They're friendly.'

'F-friendly?' squeaked Mum, as Nix and Goospa strode towards us, oozing slime across the floor.

'I wouldn't go that far,' snorted Nishi.

Goospa and Nix stopped in front of the head judge, who did not appear at all afraid to be meeting an alien from another planet.

(Like me, I suppose he was used to shocks and surprises.)

'The puny Earthling is quite right,' said Nix to the HEAD JUDGE. 'They did save your planet.'

'Save us **from what,** exactly?' he said, craning his head upwards to get a proper look at them.

HEAD JUDGE

'From the **TELEPORTATION OF EARTH** and the **DESTRUCTION OF THE GALAXY.** You would do well to thank them,' said Nix. She turned around and looked at each of us in turn. 'They have also taught me that your species is not quite as feeble-brained as I had thought.'

'Feeble-brained?' the head judge repeated incredulously.

I stifled a **giggle** and turned to the alien siblings. 'Glad to hear it. What will you do now?'

'We will **return** to Zelpha,' said Goospa. He glanced sideways at Nix. 'Is that not right, Har-Har?'

Nix hesitated for a moment; then she nodded. 'Yes, we shall. You Earthlings have made me realize that we should not run away from our problems. If you can save the galaxy, I can talk to The Pa and The Ma and *insist* they let me stand down as Crown Princess so that I can join PADRRU. I shall **NOT** run away.'

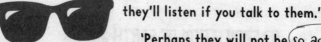

I nodded. 'Being a member of PADRRU sounds like a cool job. Almost as cool as being a **genius inventor**. I'm sure they'll listen if you talk to them.'

'Perhaps they will not be so against the idea when they hear what Goospa has to say,' said Nix. 'Perhaps it is time that Zelpha has a crown prince instead of a crown princess.'

'Or perhaps neither,' said Goospa. 'I have much to learn before such an honour is bestowed. I understand that now. We shall speak to The Pa and The Ma together. It cannot be as difficult as stopping the teleportation of

Earth, Har-Har.' He turned to Nishi. 'I believe I owe you an apology, sister of Esha-Verma-Verma-Esha.

I am _sorry_ for my behaviour.'

Berty growled at him.

'Easy, Berty,' whispered Nishi, stroking the top of his head. She scowled at Goospa. 'You shouldn't have tied us up with those smelly socks.'

'You are correct,' said Goospa. 'It was not how a prince of Zelpha should behave and I am most apologetic.' He bowed his head. 'Still, it was a pleasure to meet you, sister of Esha-Verma-Verma-Esha.' He bowed to Mum. 'Mother of Esha-Verma-Verma-Esha.' He smiled at Berty. 'Even you, peculiar creature.'

Mum made a soft whimpering noise.

'Thank you for all your help, Nix,' said Broccoli. 'Thanks for coming back for me when I was in the lava marsh.'

'And for saving my life when I was poisoned by the vilter,' said Bean.

'**Poisoned?**' squawked Mum, her eyes wide. 'Wait just a moment—'

'Thanks for getting us back to Earth,' I said over her. 'We couldn't have made it home to our families without you.'

Archibald snickered as if to say, 'Well *I* could have, but thank you for saving my humans.'

Nix blinked, a strange expression on her face, then, quite suddenly, she pulled all of us into a **slimy hug.**

'If you should ever wish to visit Zelpha, you would be *most welcome*, Earthlings,' she said, stepping away.

'Indeed you would, Har-Har,' said Goospa. 'Perhaps you could bring some blue-berries with you?'

'I am sure we can take some with us before we leave,' said Nix. 'There is a core of Earthly supplies, is there not?'

'Quite so, sister. It is called the super-market.'

Still **oozing slime**, they manoeuvred themselves around the cracks in the room, past the audience of gaping judges, who shuffled back in awe, and disappeared through the doorway.

'Don't you think you should have told them about the **KOOPLARZA?**' whispered Broccoli. He flicked a blob of slime off his arm. 'We *fried* the camouflage shields and *who knows* what else.'

'I'm sure they'll figure it out.' And they would. Nix was smart enough for anything. Almost as smart as me.

'Aliens,' said the head judge, staring at the open doorway. '**Most unexpected**.' He scratched his head. 'Why did they come here? To the HALF-CENTURY DAY?'

'They wanted the Zirboonium,' I said. 'I'm sorry about the **Brain Trophy**. I didn't mean for it to be destroyed.'

He took in the fragments of Zirboonium scattered across the floor.

'Hm,' he said.

Without a word, he collected each piece, flicking it into the ᵃⁱʳ and catching it in his palm. The Zirboonium gleamed filling me with that same

SPINGLY-TINGLY feeling

I'd felt ever since I'd first set eyes on it.

'Hm,' he said again.

A shadow of a smile twitched at the corners of his mouth.

Then he held out a piece of the **Brain Trophy** towards my DRONG of a sister.

What **ON EARTH** was he doing?

Nishi stared at the judge in bewilderment. It was the same expression she'd had on her face when I'd mistaken a cumulonimbus cloud for a cirrus.

'For you,' he said. 'You helped ꜱᴀᴠᴇ ᴛʜᴇ Eᴀʀᴛʜ, I believe?'

'I – well.' Nishi glanced at me. 'I mean, I tried. But I'm not an inventor or anything.'

The judge's eyes twinkled.

'And what is an inventor?' he said.

'I – well,' blustered Nishi. She looked at me again and I was quite certain that she was about to say that an inventor is **A REAL ANNOYING PAIN.** Instead, she shrugged. 'I think you should probably ask my sister that question.'

I flushed as the head judge looked at me.

'Well?' he said. 'What is an inventor?'

'It's – uh – someone who can – someone who . . .'

I could feel everyone, even Mum, looking at me as they waited for an answer.

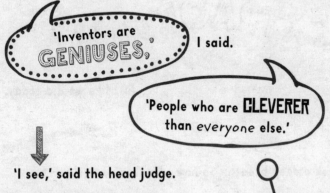

'Inventors are GENIUSES,' I said.

'People who are CLEVERER than everyone else.'

'I see,' said the head judge.

He sounded disappointed.

'At least, that's what <u>I used</u> to think.'

'Used to?'

'Yes. But actually, I don't think inventing has anything to do with being a **GENIUS** or being **SMARTER** than anyone else,' I said, the words spilling out of my mouth. 'I – I think inventing is really about seeing the world

around you differently. That's how you **INVENT**. Not by knowing the most complicated theories or mastering the most difficult formulas, but by using **ordinary things**

to make something

EXTRAORDINARY.

Just like we did today.'

I took a deep breath. 'So now I think *anyone* can be an inventor. All it takes is that special SPINGLY-TINGLY idea, a bit of **hard work** -' I glanced at Broccoli, who smiled at me and nodded – 'and **LOTS OF HELP.**'

The judge smiled, a big smile that lit up his entire face and made his eyes twinkle even brighter. 'Quite so.'

Berty wagged his tail in agreement.

'Then this is for you,' he said, holding out the fragment of Zirboonium to Nishi. 'You may not think you're an inventor, but I think anyone who saves the Earth is rather extraordinary. Don't you?'

She hesitated. I nudged her gently. 'Go on, Nishi,' I said. 'He's right. You deserve it. I don't know anyone else who would have tried to stop an alien on their own.'

'Well – I wasn't on my own,' she said. 'It was me and Berty. Isn't that right, Bert?' She stroked the top of his head. Berty **ROARED** in delight, his tail thumping the floor as she took the Zirboonium.

'For you,' said the judge, handing a fragment to Bean. 'Saviour of the Earth.'

'Did you hear that, Broccoli?' said Bean. 'Wait till I tell Mum! She's never going to believe it!'

'And you,' said the judge, holding a piece out to Broccoli.

He sniffed, his snot shaking with emotion as he took the Zirboonium and held it up to the light. The rock sparkled, its green surface shimmering like the sea on a sunny day. 'It's beautiful,' he whispered.

'And this,' said the judge. He held the last piece out to me. 'This one is for you, Esha. Thank you for saving our planet.' He stepped back and smiled at each of us in turn.

'Congratulations. You are ALL this year's Young Inventors.'

The audience whooped and cheered loudly.

'Now I must find our official photographer,' said the judge. 'We must capture this important moment!' He whipped his sunglasses onto his face, spun on his heel and hopped towards the door, his pink lab coat swishing around him. 'Everyone, please follow me to the marquees!'

I swallowed.

For years, I had DREAMT about winning The Brain Trophy.

Now – FINALLY – it had happened.

I, Esha Verma, was a Young Inventor of the Year. I turned the Zirboonium over in my hand, the rock glinting as brightly as a star from the wide, wondrous galaxy. It was even more magnificent than I had expected.

I glanced at the others around me, each of them clutching their Zirboonium pieces.

I beamed.

This might not have been how I'd imagined winning the Brain Trophy and yet, somehow, it was MILES better.

ACTU~~

THE BEST
MOMENT OF
MY ENTIRE LIFE

DINO

THE BEST MOMENT
MY ENTIRE LIFE

'Well,' said Mum. She still appeared to be recovering from the fact that she had just encountered <u>two **ALIENS**.</u> She pulled me into a hug again and kissed the top of my head.

'I'm PROUD of you, Esha.'

'You are?' I said, gawping at her.

'Yes – so <u>very proud.</u>'

'It's just that, well, I know I haven't always been the **best** daughter. I'm always *breaking* or exploding things and getting into **trouble** and—'

'And nothing,' said Mum, waving my words away. 'You are my daughter, Esha Verma, and I would **not** swap you for anyone else in all the galaxy.'

'Even if I break and explode things?'

Mum smiled. 'Even then.'

'So does that mean I'm not grounded any more? And I'm allowed to keep inventing?'

'Oh, Esha.' Her smile widened. 'Of course you can keep inventing, love. If it wasn't for your inventing, who knows what would have happened?'

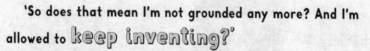

(I decided it was best not to tell her that it was, in fact, **my invention** that had got Earth in *TROUBLE* in the first place.)

'I'm so proud of you too, Nishi,' she said, hugging her. 'For working with your sister. Oh, wait till I tell your dad.

Young Inventors – both of you! He'll be delighted!' She was already pulling her phone out of her bag. 'And Aunty Usha. And Binda. They're going to be speechless!'

(I doubted that.)

'We did it,' Broccoli murmured, a ridiculous grin on his face. 'We actually won the **Brain Trophy.** I'll have loads to tell Bertha Darwin Junior when he arrives!'

I squeezed his hand. 'You're going to be a great big brother, Broccoli.'

'You really think so?' he said.

I nodded solemnly. 'I know so. Inventor's instinct, remember? Bertha Darwin Junior is going to be lucky to have you.'

'And me!' said Bean. 'Wait till he hears my story about how I became the SAVIOUR of the Earth.'

Archibald poked his head out of Bean's pocket and made a noise that sounded like, 'You and me both, *human worm*.'

'Young Inventors – yes, that's right! Yes, I know!' said Mum, shouting excitedly down the phone.

Nishi was still looking thoughtfully at her piece of Zirboonium. 'Amazing,' she said quietly.

'I know!' I said. At last, Nishi *finally understood* what I had been working towards all these years. 'I told you, didn't I? Young Inventor of the Year – it's a real *honour*, Nishi.'

'Oh that,' she said. 'Yeah, a real honour. *Actually*, I was thinking about what meteorological conditions were needed to create this kind of meteorite rock . . .'

I swapped a look with Broccoli. After everything that had happened, my DRONG of a sister was still *waffling* about the weather.

Then the two of us **started laughing**.

'What?' said Nishi. 'What's so funny?'

'Nothing,' I said, giving her a hug.

'Does this mean we're going to be invited

 to GENIE HQ?' said Broccoli,

as we headed towards the doorway.

Bean followed a few steps behind us, deep in

conversation with Archibald.

'Yup. And we get to go on the **world tour** to show

our invention to everyone . . .' I paused. 'Well, maybe not

that, considering the Inviz-Whiz got swallowed . . . but we'll

definitely get to meet other inventors around the world,'

I said. 'Just like all the other winners before us.'

'Together?' Broccoli said.

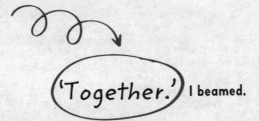

('Together.') I beamed.

And that, dear Reader, is **THE END**.

CHINA

INDIA

[A note from Broccoli: Well . . . not quite.]

ITALY

EGYPT

GREAT BARRIER REEF

But that, Reader, is a WHOLE OTHER STORY.

About the Author

Pooja Puri is an ~~expert daydreamer~~ inventor of stories. Her debut novel *The Jungle* was published by Black & White's YA imprint, Ink Road, in 2017. *The Jungle* was subsequently nominated for the 2018 CILIP Carnegie Medal. Her first middle-

grade novel, *A Dinosaur Ate My Sister*, was published in 2021 and was the first book selected for the Marcus Rashford Book Club. The sequel, *A Robot Squashed My Teacher*, was published in 2022. An Alien Stole My Pl the third in the series. She tweets @PoojaPuriWri

Here are 6 important things to know
① She likes words.
② She also likes marmalad

③ Her **TOP 3** inventions are: the telephone, the ice-cream cone and glasses.

④ She once opened a portal to another planet. Unfortunately, the portal's location is **TOP SECRET**.

⑤ She would like a pet dinosaur.

⑥ When Pooja is not inventing stories, she is working on a device that will make her invisible. It is not ready. Yet . . .

anet is

tes.

bout her: